MW00426071

A
FUNNY THING
HAPPENED ON THE
MOON

JOEY
ROGERS

A FUNNY THING HAPPENED ON THE MOON

by

Joey Rogers

Copyright © 2018 GegoDyne, LLC.

www.gegodyne.com

This is a work of fiction. Names, characters, places, and incidents either are the products of the author's imagination or are used fictitiously. Any resemblance to actual persons, living or dead, businesses, companies, events, or locales is entirely coincidental.

Cover design by Mars Dorian

ISBN: 978-1-945638-04-6

VERSION 1.0

CHAPTER 1

THE TRAINEE

"Mr. Fuentes will see you now," the receptionist said after a notification flashed on her desk.

Jeremy Scott stood and smoothed out his wrinkled uniform. He didn't know why he'd been summoned by his supervising manager, but it worried him that his presence was requested. He wished he could have prepared. He wished even more that there wasn't a meeting in the first place because he needed to be working on his project.

"This way." The receptionist motioned him to follow her down the hallway to the supervisor's office. She was a full head taller than Jeremy, and her corporate attire sharply contrasted with his trainee uniform.

"Have a seat, Mr. Scott," the manager said as Jeremy walked in. He didn't even look up from his desk.

Jeremy was too anxious to say anything, so he took a seat and waited. A meeting with a supervisor wasn't a social occasion, and he didn't think small talk would be appropriate.

Supervisor David Fuentes was a fifty-year-old, corporate lackey in charge of all senior-level trainees. He was a low-level administrator stuck in the same job for fifteen years. Managing trainees was not a desirable position at the corporation, and he was visibly worn by his tenure. The dark circles under his eyes and disheveled hair were not characteristics of an employee of his level.

The longer the silence prevailed, the more nervous Jeremy became. Fuentes swiped through several pages on his desk-display, paused to read something, and then flicked through some more. The longer Jeremy waited, the tighter he gripped the arms of his chair. His knuckles turned white. He thought that if a trainee had been this unprepared for a meeting, they would have been point-docked.

Fuentes finally let out a sigh, looked up at Jeremy, and stared at him for a long moment. "I have some bad news."

Jeremy's heart sank. "What's the problem?"

"The corporation has pulled the plug on your project."

"What?" He felt blood drained out of his face, and his stomach clenched. He had assumed there was a point-discrepancy in his bookkeeping or a new accelerated schedule he was going to have to follow. He had even considered the possibility that some prior work had cropped up. All of those scenarios would have been devastating but not as bad as what his supervisor had just said. "There must be a mistake."

"I was looking for the justification report, but I can't find one." Fuentes grimaced and returned to searching through the virtual pages on his desk.

"I'm ahead of schedule, I've reached all of my project milestones, and I've met every criteria." Jeremy's speech was rushed.

"I know." Fuentes looked up at Jeremy. "You're the top ranking senior trainee, and I've been impressed with your performance since you started your project."

Jeremy stared at the floor. "I've followed every rule and protocol without exception. How can it be canceled?"

"All I can tell you is that I received a memo notifying me that your project was canceled, and there will be no further funding." He continued flicking through pages. "There was no additional explanation, and I've spent the last hour trying to find one."

"I was under budget, and all of the simulations showed positive results." Jeremy's palms started to sweat.

"Look, I'm as surprised by this as you are." Fuentes pressed his lips together and hesitated. "I shouldn't be discussing this with you, but the corporation always provides a justification. Sometimes it isn't a very good one, but it's peculiar there is no reason at all this time."

Jeremy saw the lines in his supervisor's face as he had never seen them before. He couldn't believe his project's cancellation was stressful to someone who ruined lives for a living. "What am I supposed to do now?" His tone was bitter.

Fuentes gave up looking through the corporate records and leaned back in his chair. "You have one week to wrap up your work. The corporation expects all project resources to be liquidated, and a percentage of anything reclaimed will be deducted from your point-balance. Then, you have the option of joining another project or starting a new one."

"I won't be able to join another project in a week." Jeremy jumped out of the chair, ready to demand that he be given a valid reason for his project's cancellation. He had the right to know why. He deserved to know, but he also knew the consequences of a trainee being confrontational with a supervisor. Some rational part of his mind exerted enough influence to get him to sit back down and keep his mouth shut.

Fuentes had obviously seen odd behavior from trainees before after delivering bad news so he carried on as if Jeremy had never reacted. "Maybe you can find a project that's having difficulties." He leaned forward a bit. "You'd be an asset to any of them."

Jeremy made a barely audible snort. "You try convincing any of those losers of that." He was trying to remain respectful to his supervisor, but having the world pulled out from under him wasn't helping. "Nobody's going to share credit this late in the game. Why would they?"

"I'd be glad to speak with any of the teams on your behalf. I can even recommend a few for you to approach."

"I don't want to sound ungrateful, but why would I want to join a failing project? I would just end up with more point-debt and nothing to show for it."

Fuentes shook his head. "That's not necessarily true. Some of the teams just need a member with your talents to get them over the hump."

"The corporation can't do this to me after all I've done." Jeremy clenched his fists. "There's got to be someone else I can talk to." He believed the corporation would do the right thing if someone with decision-making power could better understand what was happening. He just needed an opportunity to explain how beneficial his project would be to the corporation.

"I'm sorry. I wish I could give you more information," Fuentes said and returned to flicking through the pages on his desk-display.

"No offense, but your being sorry isn't going to help my point-debt. Full employee status is the only way I'll ever be able to repay the corporation for my training, and I'll never get promoted without a successful project."

"Maybe your parents can help," Fuentes said.

Jeremy shook his head. "They've been gone for years, and I still have their point-debt to repay."

"If you can't start a new project, you'll have to find another team to join."

"There must be someone else I can talk to."

Fuentes look up from his desk. "There isn't."

"What if I sign a contract saying that I'll take less than the standard trainee share of any potential point-stream? Maybe they'll reconsider?"

Fuentes's tone hardened. "I've never known the corporation to reverse a decision like this."

"I'll let them have all of the credit if they just let me complete my project."

"If the corporation wanted the credit, they would just take it." His supervisor sighed. "If you find a team to join in the next week, make an appointment, and I'll get you reassigned."

Jeremy didn't know what he was going to do next, but he needed to leave his supervisor's office before he did anything that might cause him more trouble. He stood, nodded good-bye, and left. Later he realized that he forgot to close the door and would be point-docked for breaching protocol.

CHAPTER 2

THE DENT

The Launch Pad opened at 6:00 p.m., when first shift ended. Seconds after the bartender unlocked the door, Jeremy took his favorite stool at the end of the bar. He drank three quick beers to soften the edge of his impending life-change. He pondered what could have gotten his project canceled, but he failed to come up with anything. It wasn't the haze of alcohol interfering with his analysis either. He knew there wasn't anything wrong with his project. It was going to be a success, and he couldn't understand why the corporation would allow him to almost reach the finish line if they knew he would fail. They were cruel, he thought. They were unfair. Then he couldn't believe he thought such things about the corporation. They had done everything for him, and he failed them. He ordered another beer and resumed self-medicating his problems.

An hour later, Ron Newcomb entered The Launch Pad. He scanned the room and smiled when he saw a familiar face at the end of the bar and an empty stool next to it. It was the last vacant seat, and a dozen customers were standing around. "Have you seen this vid?" he asked, attempting to get Jeremy's attention.

Jeremy was focused on the lines of bubbles rising from the bottom of his beer, but he glanced up at the vid-wall to see what Ron was babbling about. "It's just another Mars mission." He returned to supervising the marching bubbles.

"They reached twenty-five hundred colonists today. One born and fifty-three delivered on the last run." Ron sat on the empty stool and swiped through the drink menu built into the surface of the bar until he found the page of Specials. He selected the cheapest item on the list without even looking to see what it was and placed his palm flat on the bar so it could read his embedded chip.

An animated circle moved out from under his hand when the payment was accepted, and a holographic image of a beer appeared on top of the circle as if it were sitting on a coaster. The projection was indistinguishable from a real beer except that it would distort if someone tried to pick it up. The technology had been perfected decades earlier and was integrated into everything, useful or not. It was even found in a dive bar.

The Launch Pad was the only drinking establishment on campus that allowed indentured employees, and Ron was a regular, though he rarely bought anything. Indentured weren't allowed to interact or congregate with the non-indentured. The corporation dictated that all indentured wear solid gray uniforms at all times and have a freshly-shaven head. They were normally thrown out of all non-work-related areas, but anyone who had the points for a drink could go to The Launch Pad. That did not, however, mean its patrons wanted to mingle with an indentured, or a dent as they were called, and Ron was glad to see Jeremy sitting in his usual spot.

The bartender brought Ron's beer and slid the glass across the bar's surface into the image of the holographic beer. The projection was supposed to deactivate when the two glasses reached parity, but the sensors needed recalibration and the gimmick no longer produced the desired effect. The bartender had to finesse the glass's position to complete the order. Nobody cared about the flashy trick, but the special effects couldn't be turned off without sacrificing the integrated order system, and The Launch Pad had no points to retain a server.

Ron lifted the amber beer to his mouth, but he stopped when the dank aroma reached his nose. "Why does the cheapest beer always have to be the bitter one?" His face wrinkled when he sampled the beverage.

"If you want alcohol, why don't you just get the powder?" Jeremy said.

Ron shook his head. "It's not the same as drinking a beer."

"Bitter is the least expensive flavor to synthesize. Don't get the cheapest one." Jeremy pointed at Ron's glass.

"I had to skip lunch to have enough points for the Special." Ron was determined to acquire a taste for the beer and took another sip.

"Then don't complain about it being bitter," Jeremy said and downed the remainder of his beer. Alcohol was his go-to vice for stress relief. Smoking was illegal and too risky, but he often visualized himself smoking. It gave him some degree of satisfaction, a virtual rush, even if he had never seen an actual cigarette outside of old vids. He really wanted one after the day's events. Instead, he placed his palm on the bar and ordered another beer while he still could.

The holographic emitter in front of Jeremy didn't work as well as the others embedded in the bar, and the image flickered so much that it garnered looks from the other clientele.

"Sorry about that," the bartender said. "I think one of the emitters is going out." He placed the drink in the exact position on his first try, and the flickering stopped.

Jeremy had put more points into beer than most of his colleagues had put into food. The daily point allotment didn't take height or weight into consideration, just seniority. Jeremy was a trainee, but he was a senior one. He was also short and thin, so his nutritional requirements could be met while still having enough points left over to curdle his liver.

Ron was the same age as Jeremy, but he was born a dent. Ron was tall, barrel-chested, and weighed over a hundred kilos. He could barely meet his nutritional requirements with his daily allotment, but that didn't stop him from splurging on a cheap beer when he could.

"Look." Ron pointed at the vid-wall. The view was of a Mars ship approaching the red planet. He smiled from ear to ear and tapped his chest with an index finger. "That's one of my engines."

"There are thousands of Mars engine rings, and they all look exactly alike." Jeremy rolled his eyes.

"See the striations on the top segment of the third ring? There was a glitch in my fabricator last year, and it made that pattern on the outer shell. I fabricated two rings before the problem was resolved."

Jeremy grimaced. "And they let something defective go all the way to Mars?"

"It passed all of the tests. They weren't going to scrap that many points and fabrication hours because of some weird rendering artifact."

"The Mars missions must be desperate to use defective equipment."

"They need all of the engines they can get. Mars Colony is gaining momentum and will reach a pop of twenty-five thousand in the next ten years," Ron said.

Jeremy looked down at his beer. "Why would anyone want to go to Mars?" He was negative to all things Mars because they were competitors to his own lunar engine project.

"I'd go in a heartbeat, but they're not going to relocate an indentured fabricator."

"They'll need fabricators there at some point. Your dream may one day come true," Jeremy said sarcastically.

"They'll have their own techs to run them. They'll never give up the points to retrain me for different equipment much less transfer me to another planet. Besides, Mars has its own indentured population."

"Bob, can you change the vid to something other than fucking Mars?" Jeremy asked, but the bartender ignored him.

"You're just cranky because your project was canceled."

Jeremy choked on the beer he had just swallowed and coughed a few times. "How do you know that?"

"Nobody pays any attention to what they say around the fabricators. We're all indentured," Ron said. "Why did they cancel your project?"

"I don't know. They wouldn't tell me."

Ron's eyes grew wide. "Wow. They should've told you something."

"There hasn't been a project canceled since I've been in the training program." Jeremy coughed again and cleared his throat.

"I thought you trainees flunked out of the program all the time."

"Washing out on your own merit is a wholly different thing from the corporation stepping in and terminating your project."

"I guess it's better to be canceled than fail out." Ron took another drink of his beer and wrinkled his nose.

"Not completing your project is failure. It doesn't matter what the reason is." Jeremy looked down at his beer.

"I think if it were me, I'd rather have my project canceled than be a flunky."

"Successfully completing my project was the only way I could repay the corporation for my training. I'm screwed."

"I bet you will come up with an even better idea for your next project."

"I thought dents couldn't gamble, and my lunar engine was the best idea I've ever had."

"That's because it's the only thing you've thought about for the last four years."

"If I can't join another project in a week, I'll have to sell myself into indenturehood to keep from getting fired. My life is over." Jeremy paused for a split second. "No offense."

"You just have to change your focus from the Moon to Mars, and you'll get picked right back up. It's not like you're one of those flunkies."

"All of my research is for short-range, near-body transit. There's not enough gravity between Earth and Mars for my prototype engine to operate."

"Then you may have to change your field of research. You just have to think *Mars*." Ron pointed back at the vid-wall, which was showing the planet again.

"I've spent the last four years thinking *Moon*. I'll double my debt if I start over with something new—if I can even come up with something new. Besides, the corporation will never loan me the points to start over." Jeremy frowned.

"Can't you use your engine to go from Mars to its moons?"

Jeremy laughed. "There are fewer people wanting to go to Phobos and Deimos than Earth's moon. Besides, they're not large enough for my engine to work."

Ron leaned over and patted Jeremy on the back. "You'll figure something out."

Jeremy chugged the rest of his beer. "Why does someone whose life is more of a shit pile than mine have to be so fucking optimistic?"

"It's not hard to be optimistic at the bottom. Everything's better, and you don't have the exclusive on wanting a better life, even if it's something I'll never obtain."

"You live in a delusion." Jeremy slowly shook his head.

"But it's a good delusion," Ron said with a laugh. "How many have you had?"

"I've lost count." Eight circles illuminated on the bar's surface in front of Jeremy.

Ron puckered his lips and let out a long whistle. "Too many." Then he braced himself for another sip of his own.

"Give me a break," Jeremy said. "My pathetic life is over."

CHAPTER 3

THE IDEA

Jeremy didn't have time for friends, so he didn't consider Ron one. On the other hand, Ron thought Jeremy was one of his best friends, mostly because all indentured considered each other as family and Jeremy was the only non-indentured who didn't treat Ron like he had the plague.

Early in his training, Jeremy learned that the best way to gain information about fabricating engine rings was to ask a lot of questions about how it was actually done. The better he understood the limits and quirks of the process, the better he could design his new propulsion system. The ones who could answer his questions weren't the corporate stooges giving seminars on the topic; they were the ones who actually did the fabrication. Jeremy had only been a trainee for a week when he found the one dent brave enough to hang out at The Launch Pad, and it just so happened that the dent was a fabricator.

"Aren't you fabricating one of the Mars engines right now?" Jeremy asked.

"One of them. Twenty-four rings are currently being rendered at this campus," Ron said.

Jeremy straightened his posture and turned to look at Ron. "How long does it take to complete one?"

"It depends on the model, but the latest specs take about a month. Sixty twelve-hour shifts."

"And they're ten-meter rings?"

"Ten-meter diameter, thirty-one point four linear meters." Ron raised his eyebrows. "Why are you suddenly interested in Mars engines?"

"What if I only wanted to render a one-meter ring?"

Ron shook his head. "That wouldn't have the capacity to do anything useful. You'd need at least seven meters to achieve net thrust."

"Short-range, near-body. Remember? I can use a one-meter ring to carry a craft and fifty kilos of cargo to the Moon."

Ron tilted his head. "Maybe that's why your project was canceled."

"Why?"

"Nobody believes it'll work."

"It'll work."

Ron slowly shook his head.

"My engine doesn't work like the Mars engines, and the simulations show it'll work." Jeremy pulled out his display-card to show Ron the data.

Ron nodded as he looked through the information.

"See?" Jeremy said.

"If the corporation could use smaller engine rings, they would already be doing it. Shaving off just one meter would save them millions of points."

Jeremy took in a deep breath. "You're not listening. It won't work for Mars. It has to be a near-body system like the Earth and Moon."

"If you say so." Ron wrinkled up his face in anticipation of his next sip of his beer.

Jeremy's mind raced down a path he hadn't previously considered. "How long would it take to fabricate one?"

"What?" Ron's eyebrows raised.

"A one-meter ring."

Ron sat his beer back down on the bar. "Depending on how we can stack the segments in the rendering plane…it could probably be done in less than a shift if it was the only thing being rendered."

Jeremy's eyes got wider. "Could you make a few segments here and there over several days without being noticed?"

"First of all, that would be stealing from the corporation. An indentured employee caught stealing is fired without question. Second, all of the raw materials are metered to the job. While I might be able to run a few extra segments, I wouldn't have the inputs to produce them. Third—"

Jeremy interrupted. "Say there were some defective runs. Instead of throwing them away, I would take them away for you."

"All defects are sent to recycling. Superconductive materials have a high point-value. There's also a special team to investigate why there was a problem."

"How much material would you need to fabricate a one-meter ring?"

"It'll depend on your segment's core diameter."

"Twenty-five centimeters."

"I would have to run it through the rendering system with your exact specs, but I'd guess it would need a hundred kilos of raw materials or so."

Jeremy turned back to the bar and took another gulp from his beer. "That's a lot of points that I don't have."

"If you only have a twenty-five-centimeter core, it could probably be run alongside a scheduled job. The rendering chamber is cylindrical, and the Mars engine segments are rectangular. That leaves some space to work with on the rendering plane."

Jeremy was watching the bubbles in his beer again, but he was still listening to Ron. "Wouldn't that slow down the fabrication?"

"The rendering time is based on the number of slices. The amount of material used for each slice doesn't matter unless your layer density is greater than the primary job."

"It will work with the same layer density as the Mars segments." Jeremy's mind went even deeper down a path that he had never previously explored. "We just need to get the material." He bit his lip as he thought about ways to acquire it.

"I think you'll need at least twenty-five to fifty-thousand points worth of materials, and even then, it would be pretty risky."

Jeremy's excitement soured on his face. "I know. It's risky to even think such things, and I'm not one to break the rules."

Ron paused for a second. "I'd be willing to do it if you can get the material."

Jeremy looked at him with raised eyebrows. "You do realize what getting fired means?"

"I have no desire to be executed by the corporation," Ron said as he rubbed the back of his neck.

"If you fabricate the engine, I can send my prototype spacecraft to the Moon. The corporation would have to take my project seriously and recognize the potential point-stream."

"That's a great idea, but you'll never get the points for the raw materials."

"I know," Jeremy said and frowned. "I would have to steal them. I wouldn't even know how to start planning that." He was building himself up for another failure, and he knew it. "I shouldn't have to work this hard to prove my worth to the corporation." His chin dropped.

"Maybe you can find a different department to fund your project. Propulsion can't be the only one interested in going to the Moon."

"Nobody wants to go to the Moon. It has a bad reputation. That was a risk I accepted when I started the project."

"Really? Why?" Ron asked.

"It's because of that whole fake Moon landing thing a hundred and fifty years ago. Nobody ever tried to go back."

"Nobody's been to the Moon?" Ron gave Jeremy an incredulous stare. "How is that possible? We've made hundreds of trips to Mars. I just assumed we'd been to the Moon, and there wasn't anything there."

"They've sent probes, but no people," Jeremy said.

"If nobody wants to go to the Moon," Ron said, "you're going to have to do a much better job of selling me on why your project is worth the risk."

Jeremy threw his shoulders back and said with a gleam in his eyes, "Because my engine will be the cheapest, most efficient means of interplanetary travel ever conceived."

Ron blinked rapidly. "That's quite a claim."

"The only downside is that my engine only works within the Earth-Moon system."

"Is it really interplanetary travel if you're just going to the Moon?" Ron asked with a grin.

"The Moon's bigger than Pluto." Jeremy furrowed his brow.

"That's not helping your argument."

"Ganymede and Titan are both larger than Mercury."

"But you're not going to Ganymede or Titan."

"It's transitive." Jeremy pressed his lips together. "How many points does it take to get a kilo to Mars?"

"Fifty thousand points per kilo. It's going down though. It'll be forty thousand before the population breaks 10K."

"I can get to the Moon for under ten points per kilo, and most of that cost will be for the launch-drone, not the space-craft itself."

Ron laughed. "That's impossible."

"Not to mention that the lunar rings are significantly smaller and therefore cheaper to build than a Mars ring."

"If they work." Ron snorted.

"On top of that, I can use rechargeable power packs to run them, and I don't need a costly fusion reactor. The only cost after fabrication is maintenance, and charging will be done with solar panels. It's completely reusable, scalable, and eco-friendly."

"So, it's cheaper, what else?"

"Earth and Mars only line up to create an optimal launch window every two years. The interplanetary distance can range from 50 million to 400 million kilometers making schedules erratic. On the other hand, the Moon has an opti-mal launch window every day with a constant 384,400 kilo-meter travel distance."

"You're getting better at selling it, but why would I want to go to the Moon instead of Mars?"

"Cheap transit to the Moon would open up a whole new lunar mining industry and drastically simplify all cislunar operations. It would even make the Moon a viable candidate for colonization."

"What can you mine on the Moon?"

"Aluminum, magnesium, silicon, oxygen, iron. There are trace elements as well. Any material mined on Mars will only be useful to Mars. It will always be too expensive to transport any of that material back to Earth. With my system, bringing material back to Earth can be done for virtually no points."

Ten minutes later, Jeremy was still going on about the benefits his lunar engine would bring to the corporation. Ron finally interrupted, "Has it ever occurred to you that the corporation would've already gone to the Moon if it was worthwhile?"

"They just didn't have my engine," Jeremy countered. "My project will make it a point-positive endeavor."

Spurred on by his alcohol content and aroused techno-bravado, Jeremy's volume had increased enough for his conversation with Ron to be overheard. To most, babbling about theoretical lunar transit was a waste of time, but there was one person at the bar listening to every word Jeremy said.

CHAPTER 4

THE BACKER

Theodor Rufus Davenport VII was sitting at the opposite end of the bar from Jeremy and Ron. Theo had no desire to be at The Launch Pad. He needed aristocratic cocktails to flaunt and servants to attend to him. He also needed a buffer between him and the nearest commoner. None of his requirements could be met at a dive bar, but he understood that sacrifices had to be made if he wanted to get what he desired.

Technically, Theo was a trainee, no different from Jeremy. He had more seniority in the training program, but that wasn't what made him exceptional. It was the fact that Theo's father was the CEO of the corporation. That not-so-minor detail elevated Theo's status to a category of its own, and he didn't miss any opportunity to reap the benefits of his birthright.

Theo was not, however, particularly gifted when it came to original thinking or idea germination. He didn't grasp the science or mathematics behind the technologies he needed to master in order to complete a successful project, and he was stuck being a trainee. It was his tenth year in the program. His abundance of points and top-level connections didn't help him either. He needed to impress the corporate board and his father if he ever wanted to run the corporation, and he had to do it before his younger brothers overtook him on the career ladder.

Theo rudely pushed his way between Jeremy and Ron. "Pardon me."

Jeremy looked up from his beer to see who it was. Theo was tall and looked like a younger version of his father. Most trainees were intimidated by his presence, but Jeremy wasn't. "Isn't this place a little beneath you?"

"Absolutely, and so are you." Theo smirked.

"Then what do you want?" Jeremy knew what kind of person Theo was. Everyone did.

"I overheard the conversation you were having with the dent," he said with as much disgust as he could infuse into the last word.

"Hi, I'm Ron." He offered to shake hands.

Theo ignored the introduction and focused solely on Jeremy. "I want in on your project."

"My project was canceled."

"Everyone knows that," Theo said, "but I can get you around that minor detail."

"Why would you want in on my project?" Jeremy made no attempt to hide his skepticism.

"Mars is so blasé. I need to be involved with something more original, and a lunar project is different."

Jeremy wasn't inebriated enough to dismiss the possibility of getting some assistance from Theo, but he had to explore whether or not the offer was legitimate. It was more likely that he was just building up the hopes of a plebe so he could grind him back into the ground with his heel. "You don't know anything about my project."

"I know more than you think." Theo smirked again.

"How could you possibly help? From what I understand, you're not particularly capable when it comes to actually *helping* on a project." Jeremy had heard horror stories of how Theo moved in on a project, took over, never did any work, and blamed everyone else when it failed.

"Are you able to send cargo to the Moon for less than ten points per kilo?"

"Yes, I just have to prove it with a test flight."

"So, prove it." Theo crossed his arms and waited for Jeremy's reply.

"My project was canceled before I could complete the spacecraft."

"Why was your project canceled?"

"I wasn't told."

Theo thought for a second. "It's probably because the Takata Corporation has invested all of its points into Mars mining expeditions and bought up all of the mining rights."

"And you think the corporation canceled my project because I don't help them compete with Takata?" Jeremy wasn't privy to what went on between competing corporations, but Theo's speculation was a plausible reason for his project's cancellation.

"Yes," Theo said, "and a new point-stream that isn't dependent on Mars would be of value to the corporation."

"If the corporation was interested in that, they wouldn't have canceled my project." Jeremy drank the remainder of his beer and pushed the empty glass away.

"Their decisions are always point-based. It's just a formula, and your project didn't hit the marks. Probably because it's too different from the run-of-the-mill Mars drudgery."

Jeremy's eyebrows shot up. "What exactly would you be able to provide?" He regretted asking after the words left his mouth because he had just opened a door that he might not be ready for.

"I can provide the raw materials you need."

Jeremy wrinkled his brow. "You don't even know how much I need."

"A hundred kilograms."

Jeremy paused trying to figure out how Theo knew that but decided to go along and see how far he could get. "Yes, at least a hundred kilos. Fifty-thousand points worth."

"And?" Theo snarkily asked.

"And, that's a lot of points."

"Maybe to someone like you."

"What are you wanting in return?"

"I want some of your project credit."

Jeremy snorted. "I'm not giving you credit for my engine design."

"It doesn't have to be for the design, but it must have a technical aspect. One that is essential to its success and satisfies my final training requirements."

"Funding is essential," Jeremy said.

"It has to be technical."

"Can you do planetary navigation?" Jeremy was hoping there was something Theo could actually contribute to the project.

Theo laughed. "Do you want to actually get to the Moon?"

"Then what can you do?"

"I'll leave that up to you. It doesn't matter to me as long as it's technical in nature and doesn't require my involvement."

"You get me the raw materials, Ron will run my engine alongside the Mars engine fabrication, and I'll launch my prototype spacecraft to the Moon with a transmitter."

"I can't just—" Ron started, but Jeremy held up his hand to stop him.

"Your proposal isn't good enough." Theo shook his head. "If you want my support, the spacecraft must also return to Earth."

"That was never part of my project," Jeremy said in a higher than normal pitch.

"It has to be, or you haven't really accomplished anything."

"It'll prove we can go to the Moon with minimal inputs."

"We can do that with a railgun and a guidance pack."

"You can't deliver cargo with a railgun."

"But I can deliver a transmitter with one," Theo countered.

"The project's test flight was only for a one-way trip." Jeremy knew Theo had a point, but he would have never gotten the corporation to fund a round trip with an untested engine design.

"You'll have to update your plan if you want my support."

"It'll take me some time, and I'll probably need two engine rings instead of one, which will double the material requirements."

"I'll give you two days to revise your plan. I'll make my final decision after I review it."

"That's not enough time to re-engineer the whole project for a round trip."

"Call my assistant and set up an appointment." Theo placed his palm on the bar. A virtual business card appeared as a hologram floating in midair.

Jeremy waved his hand through the card to download the information into his embedded chip.

"If you don't come up with something convincing," Theo said, "have fun being a dent." He turned and gave Ron an impudent look and left.

"Are you able to return the spacecraft back to Earth?" Ron asked as soon as Theo was outside the bar.

"In theory." Jeremy twisted his lips.

"I'll get fired if I get caught fabricating the parts," Ron said. "Fired," he slowly repeated.

"You were the one who was just volunteering to help."

"I know, but that's when I thought you couldn't get the points for the materials."

"I'll split any points that come out of it with you."

"You know indentured can't accept points."

"I'll find some way to pay you back," Jeremy said, ignoring the risk Ron would be taking. "We're going to have to get a navigator though."

"How did Theo overhear our conversation? You were pretty loud and all, but he wasn't standing next to us, and it's noisy in here."

"The bastard has implants." Jeremy stuck a finger in his ear.

Ron's eyebrows shot up. "That would be a pretty high-tech implant. Wouldn't it?"

Jeremy shrugged. "Points are no object for people like him."

"That's pretty creepy," Ron said.

Jeremy ran his hands through his hair. "I've never gone against the corporation like this."

"You're too big a stickler for corporate protocol."

"That's how you succeed," Jeremy said with conviction.

Ron let out a defeated laugh. "How's that working for you?"

Jeremy ignored Ron's question. His mind was already re-configuring his design to make a round trip.

CHAPTER 5

THE DECISION

Jeremy and Ron stayed another hour at The Launch Pad after Theo left. Jeremy spent most of that time trying to convince Ron that his risk was minimal if he helped with the fabrication. An ember of hope glowed in Jeremy. If he had to fan it at Ron's expense, so be it, he thought. Ron had spent his entire life indentured, and it wasn't in his nature to say no. Jeremy knew he could leverage that trait.

Jeremy stumbled out of the bar in a hybrid state. There was giddiness over the possibility of actually realizing his project and enabling him to eliminate his debt. There was also paranoid disbelief that some super-rich asshole would pony up the points to prevent his downhill slide into indentured servitude. The two states should have canceled each other out, but they didn't.

Jeremy went to the senior project barracks where he lived. He entered a partitioned, three-by-three meter cubicle and slid a semi-opaque door shut behind him. Privacy was somewhat of an illusion. The walls were only a meter-and-a-half tall, and residential cubicles were on all sides but the one adjacent to the corridor. His cube was fairly luxurious compared to others, though he'd lived in much worse conditions. Ron had the same sized cube but shared it with four others. Some lower-level dents even used a hot bunking system.

Unlike Jeremy's colleagues who covered their living space with countless tchotchkes and decorations, his was bare except for a vintage postcard stuck to the wall. It was from 1946 and had been encased in an airtight protective sleeve. It had been his mother's prize possession and was the only thing he had left of his parents.

The postcard depicted three small sailboats with colorful sails, two red and one yellow. They were sailing off the coast of a green shoreline with gentle mountains in the background. The water was calm, but the sails were full. Cheerful occupants were riding to some destination of their choosing. Jeremy was jealous of their picturesque lives in a place called Ocean Grove, New Jersey. He didn't know if it was even a real place, but it didn't matter to him. The back of the postcard had a handwritten message from Zelda telling her friend Amy how she was enjoying her summer. She had composed an entire fantasy tale condensed into a few sentences, and Jeremy knew the message by heart.

Jeremy couldn't sleep, and it wasn't because of the four different vids playing on the neighboring walls or the lights that wouldn't be turned off for another ten minutes. The scale in his mind was weighing his options, and it teetered back and forth. He could only hope for some miraculous solution to come along in the next week before he was completely locked out of his project, or he could risk working with Theo to complete it. Jeremy cringed just at the thought of working with Theo.

If Jeremy did nothing, he wouldn't be able to repay his debt and would become indentured. Contrary to Supervisor Fuentes's optimistic suggestion of finding another project to join, that option was a long shot. Even if he could find one, he would get minimal credit and a fraction of any potential point-stream it generated, and he would still end up being indentured. If he accepted Theo's offer and the mission failed, the result would be the same. He closed his eyes and took in a deep breath. His only chance was to work with Theo and successfully complete the mission.

CHAPTER 6

THE PITCH

At 5:00 a.m., the lights snapped on in the project barracks. A bell rang to make sure everyone was awake. It had a mechanical clapper and was obnoxiously loud, but Jeremy wasn't asleep. He'd spend the entire night updating his engine design to make a round trip.

Mars engine fabrication generated a healthy point-stream for the corporation and was a shiny jewel in the corporate crown. Over 50 percent of the campus was dedicated to their manufacturing. Ron worked in the Large-Scale Fabrication Facility, which was devoted solely to the creation of the Mars engine rings. The industrial bays housed twenty-four large-scale extrusion fabricators. They created their product one molecular layer at a time through a process of graviton-based stereolithography. As the accumulated material was pushed out a port in the rear of the machine, it gave the appearance of extrusion. A misnomer, but an accurate description of what the process looked like.

Ron was a level-three fabrication engineer, the highest rating an indentured employee could achieve. His job was to take the plans from a designer, optimize them for the fabricator, and produce the product with minimal resources. He was overqualified for the job, but because of that, he was able to do a better job than all his co-workers. Jeremy was fully aware of Ron's capabilities. If anyone could surreptitiously slide another design into the fabricator without anyone knowing, it would be Ron.

The Large-Scale Fabrication Facility was a secure facility. Entrance required an ID chip embedded in the employee's hand, and there had to be a valid reason for entry. Jeremy's project only granted him access to Project Rendering, a neighboring facility, which contained smaller fabricators. A year earlier, while scavenging for parts, Jeremy had discovered a maintenance shaft connecting the two facilities. He'd never had a use for it until now.

"Ron," Jeremy said.

Ron jumped. He'd never had a visitor before. "How did you get in here?"

"Maintenance shaft," Jeremy said as if he had entered the facility every day.

"You're going to get me fired. Nobody can see you here with me." Ron got up from his console and looked down the corridor to see if anyone could have seen Jeremy.

"I passed a dozen fabricators on the way here. Not one of them paid any attention to me."

"That's because you didn't stop and chat with them." Ron continued to look around.

"I'm not here to chat. I'm here to plan for our meeting with Theo." Jeremy pulled a display-card from his pocket.

Ron sighed. "If you haven't noticed, I'm working. I'll be off at six." He returned to his console and checked the readouts.

"We have to recruit a navigator tonight, so we have to do our planning now."

Ron frowned. "I have to do my job now."

"You can do both."

Ron rubbed the back of his neck. "I'll get docked for any faults that occur during my run."

"You're fabricating the same engine you've done for the last how many years?"

"Three years, but that doesn't matter. If I screw up a run, it's not going to cost you anything."

"You're wrong," Jeremy said in a serious tone. "It would cost me a fabricator, and I've only got one to choose from."

"Gee, thanks. I'm glad to know I'm indispensable." The control panel started flashing red and beeping. Ron jerked back around to the panel and made some adjustments. "See, you're already causing me to mess up."

"That was just a supply feed issue. Minor."

"I'm going to face the control panel while you distract me."

"I don't need you to look at me, just listen and see if you can figure out how much raw material we actually need to build my engine."

"Do you have the new design specs?"

"I finished the modifications this morning. I had to add a second engine ring for the return trip."

"If you could already get to the Moon with one ring, why do you need a second?"

"One-sixth gravity on the lunar surface drastically reduces the launch capability, and there's no launch-drone to assist on the Moon."

"Shouldn't it be easier to get off the Moon than Earth?"

"Not when your propulsion is based on defected gravity."

"Are you sure your new benefactor's going to be in for that degree of pointage?"

Jeremy clenched his jaw. "I have to assume he's not concerned about the points."

"It may be close to a hundred thousand."

"He's the one who said we had to make a round trip."

"Are you sure your engine's going to make it there and back?"

Jeremy looked down at the floor. "I was a lot surer when I was just going to have to get there."

"What about all of the other components?"

"I already have the capsule completed. It's a second-hand, graphene shell."

"Power?"

"I used the point-bonus for reaching my last milestone to purchase a set of used power pack modules."

"How used?"

"They can reach 85 percent capacity. I've also been collecting solar-sheeting fragments from the Mars missions for

43

two years. They usually just throw them away because they can't be recycled without contaminating the substrate. It's a lovely mosaic of mismatched tiles but it'll do, unless you can fabricate me some new ones?"

"You can't use a large-scale fabricator to make solar-sheeting," Ron said, knowing that Jeremy knew that too.

"It doesn't matter. I've got enough surface area to charge my power packs—it just takes a little longer."

"What about comm and telemetry?"

"I have them. I've been repairing rejected parts from the component graveyard."

"Anything else?"

"I'm going to get a sample collector since the spacecraft is now returning to Earth."

"And that's all?"

"There is one thing, and it may be difficult to acquire."

Ron turned around to look at Jeremy. "And what is that?"

"The navigator."

"You know a navigator who will be glad to help." A smug grin covered Ron's face.

"If I ask for a favor, it might be interpreted in an unintended way."

"No, it'll be interpreted in a very specific way." Ron chuckled.

CHAPTER 7

THE NAVIGATOR

Alice Porchetta was beautiful, but not in an ascetic way. She was only seen for what she was able to do with her mind. She wasn't unattractive by any means, but her appearance was not what drew people to her. Instead, they were blinded by her brilliance and couldn't see past it. She possessed the uncanny ability to process numbers and equations in her head so quickly and accurately that she could easily outperform a general-purpose computer. Unlike her electronic competitors, she could also dynamically adjust her calculations and compare suites of variables, formulas, and parameters to evolve her solutions. She could always come up with a better solution than any computer short of an industrial strength AI. Even then, she could still compete.

Alice didn't know how she could do what she did with mathematics. She could just do it, and she had always been able to. She wasn't fun to play cards with—or any game that could be skewed with mathematics—because she would always win. She also found that the more she practiced her talent, the more she could do, and she had been practicing as long as she could remember.

Alice grew up in a point-positive world. Her father was a mid-level executive in the human resources department, so her family could easily afford her corporate training. She had been ostracized as a child because of her talent and had problems relating to other kids. They didn't understand her, and she didn't understand them. Nevertheless, she turned out to be a level-headed, likable person even if she was the smartest person in the room wherever she went. She did have problems making friends, since everyone was intimidated by her abilities.

Alice had outpaced her colleagues in a short time and had already earned a top-level certification in mathematics and computational science. She was smarter than the trainers, so there was no reason to waste her talents sitting in useless sessions when she could be generating points for the corporation. She was considered a full employee, but her abbreviated training earned her a probationary status.

The corporation had been planning to exploit Alice ever since she joined the training program. It just hadn't figure out how to apply her talents to reap the most points. She was rotated through various departments to see how they could benefit from her presence, and she had been extremely successful in all of them. Until a niche was carved out for her, she was free to study and develop her abilities, as long as she contributed to the corporation's bottom line.

Jeremy and Alice joined the training program in the same quarter and had attended several of the same sessions together. Jeremy treated Alice like a normal person. He was always focused on eliminating his point-debt, and this self-centered distraction had the effect of making Alice feel less like the star attraction of a freak show.

Over time, it became obvious to Jeremy, and everyone else, that he had somehow garnered more interest from Alice than was expected from a colleague. Alice didn't hide her interest, and she casually asked him to dinner and other functions at the corporation. He didn't have time for friends, much less romance or a relationship. Those activities were for the point-positive. He also believed that since they were from totally different social and economic strata, anything between them would be awkward. The awkwardness resulted anyway.

CHAPTER 8

THE COFFEEHOUSE

After Ron's shift, he and Jeremy met outside a coffee-house off the main corridor running through the corporate campus. Jeremy knew Alice would be there. He knew her schedule as well as she did because he wanted to avoid accidental meet-ups. Alice also followed a perfectly mapped-out schedule with mathematical precision, making it fairly easy to determine her whereabouts.

As the two entered the old-style coffeehouse, a bell on the door jingled and several people turned to see who entered, including Alice.

"There she is," Ron said.

"She's seen us," Jeremy said and quickly looked down to avoid making eye contact.

"It smells so good in here." Ron inhaled deeply. "I've never had coffee."

"If we're successful, I'll buy you one."

"They'll throw me out of here long before we get to that." Ron gave a wry smile.

Jeremy shook his head. "Nobody enforces segregation, especially in a place like this." He headed straight for Alice's table with Ron in tow.

Alice cupped a large, half-full cappuccino between her hands. A display-card was propped up on the table, and its screen was filled with a myriad of equations and three-dimensional graphs.

"Hi, Alice," Jeremy said. It felt like his cheeks were flushed, but he hoped it was just his imagination.

"Hello." She sat her cappuccino down on the table. "What are you doing here?"

"Looking for you."

"Really?" Her posture stiffened. She knew Jeremy avoided her, and she was immediately suspicious about his presence, but getting to interact with him had already made her day.

"You know Ron, don't you?" He leaned his head in Ron's direction.

She smiled at Ron. "I've seen you at The Launch Pad."

"I haven't seen you there in quite a while," Jeremy said.

"This place is more my style."

"I can see why." Ron was still taking in at all of the things he had never seen before.

"I have a proposal for you," Jeremy said.

"To go out on a date?" She thought it couldn't hurt to put that option out there. She also wanted to needle Jeremy for his engineered avoidance of her.

"No." He lowered his eyes for a split second. "I need your help on my project."

Her enthusiastic expression was dampened but not gone. "I thought your project had been canceled."

"How do you know that?" Jeremy was beginning to wonder if he had a sign on his back advertising his most humiliating setback.

"News travels fast," she said.

Jeremy thought she must be following his activities more closely than he had previously imagined.

An older woman in a coffeehouse staff uniform came up to Ron and said in a contemptuous tone, "I'm sorry, but you'll have to leave. No dents allowed."

Ron wasn't surprised by the request and was already turning to leave when Alice intervened. "He's with me." She motioned both Jeremy and Ron to have a seat at the table.

"If you're sure, Miss Porchetta," the lady said with a disgusted look on her face. She didn't want any indentured in the coffeehouse, but she didn't want to risk upsetting Alice either. Both Jeremy and Ron took a seat at the small table, and the woman left.

"My project was canceled, but I'm still going to build the engine and run the mission."

"How can I help with that?" She picked up her cappuccino and took a sip.

"I need a planetary navigator."

"If your project's been canceled, why are you running the mission?"

"I'm going to prove to the corporation that it works and will generate a valuable point-stream."

Alice raised an eyebrow. "Isn't it risky to go against the corporation like that? Why not just start over with a new project?"

"Because I don't have the points to start over. I'll have to sell myself to the corporation just to pay back what I already owe."

"Why would the corporation listen to you after breaking protocol?"

"They won't be able to turn down the potential points."

"Maybe." Alice sat her cup down on the table. "But that seems like a pretty big assumption to me."

"Do you think I'm crazy for even trying to complete my project?" Jeremy was starting to have an uneasy feeling that his plan for redemption might not be as viable as he thought.

"I didn't say that," she quickly replied. "But you need to look at this realistically. You could make your situation worse."

"How can it be worse than becoming indentured?" Jeremy realized what he had just said and gave Ron an apologetic look. He was quiet for a moment as he considered what Alice had said, but his innate drive to finish the project, no matter what kicked in. "I know my project will work. If the corporation sees my success, they'll have to get on board. Besides, I have nothing to lose, and this is the only way I can keep from being indentured."

Alice didn't think in terms of point-debt or risk of being indentured, but she could empathize with Jeremy's problem.

She also wanted more than anything to be the one who helped Jeremy be successful. "What can I do to help?"

"I need a navigator who can handle non-standard specs and theoretical engine profiles."

"What makes you think I can do that?" Alice never flaunted her abilities, even when it was the best leverage she had with Jeremy.

Jeremy smiled. "I know what you're capable of."

"There are a dozen project teams that could plot a course to the Moon."

"And back," Ron added.

"But there's only one person who can do it without a nav-unit," Jeremy said.

"Why don't you have a nav-unit?" she asked.

"Because I don't have the points for one. Will you do it?" Jeremy rocked in placed while he waited for a reply.

"I don't think you've ever asked me for anything before. Why now?" Her eyebrows raised.

"I'll be honest. I'm desperate. This is the only chance I have to get the corporation to see the value of my project, and you're the only person I have any hope of convincing to help."

"Why? Because nobody has wanted to go to the Moon for a hundred and fifty years?" She instantly regretted suggesting that Jeremy's project might not be worthy of his efforts.

"Because my project was canceled, I have no points, nobody believes my engine will work, *and* nobody wants to go to the Moon."

"If you don't have enough points for a nav-unit, you don't have enough points to fabricate the engine."

"Ron's going to do the fabrication, and I may have a patron."

"A patron?" she said drawing out the word. "Who's going to do that?" She held up her hand. "No offense."

"You know him." Jeremy paused as he felt a rush of embarrassment pass over him. "Theo Davenport."

She laughed. "He would never help you." She laughed some more. "You're not the kind of person he wants to be associated with. Again, no offense."

"I know that, but he needs project credit on his vita if he ever wants to be promoted out of the trainee program. Besides, he's the one who approached me."

"He's an opportunist, but why would he want to get in on a canceled lunar project when everyone else is focused on Mars?"

"Theo said Takata bought up all of the mining rights on Mars. That blocks the corporation from a huge point-stream. If I can get my spacecraft finished and complete a trip to the Moon and back right now, the lost mining rights become irrelevant. I'm in the right place at the right time to save the corporation's ass with an alternative point-stream."

"Does Theo know any of this for certain? Or is he just telling you that?"

"I'm sure he's speculating to some degree, but he has access to higher-level information than I do."

Alice slowly shook her head. "I don't think you can trust Theo."

"I know we can't really trust him, but if he's willing to fork over the points to get the engine built, I have to take the risk."

Alice sat up straight in her chair. "How are you going to get clearance to launch?"

"I had already planned on performing a launch-drone test, and I have a certificate for that. I'll just launch during the test."

"They will surely detect that you launched something to the Moon."

"All eyes are on Mars. If timed right, we can launch with the Moon in opposition."

"What if we're caught?" she asked.

"I won't tell them you're involved. Even if you were connected to us, they aren't going to punish their wunderkind." He looked down at the table.

"They might," she said. "The corporation hasn't figured out what they're going to do with me, so nothing is certain about my future here."

"I don't think you have to worry. You're an asset to the corporation. I'm not. They'll punish the one responsible if it comes to that."

"What do I get out of this?" she asked.

"I'll split any points I get out of it with you."

"I'm not interested in your points." Her tone was dismissive.

"You can share in the credit."

"I don't really care about credit either."

"I don't have anything else to offer," Jeremy said. Ron kicked his leg under the table.

"You can go out on a date with me," Alice calmly said.

There was an awkward silence as Jeremy's mind raced to find a way out of the trap. "I will if we're successful," he finally said. He had already sold out to the devil to get funding, what difference would a date make? He thought his chances for success weren't that great anyway.

"Are you sure your engine will be able to get to the Moon and back?"

"The simulations show it will; however, I was originally planning for a one-way trip. Theo said it had to return to Earth to get his contribution."

"Which is what?" she asked.

"He's providing the raw materials for the fabrication. I have everything else."

"You have to go on a date if you're successful or not." She took a sip of her cappuccino.

"If we're not successful, I'll be indentured."

"That's not a problem," she said. "We'll do it before your retirement."

Jeremy tried to change the subject. "I have to present a plan to Theo tomorrow night. Will you come with us?"

"I'll go, but I'd like to see the engine specs and verify your simulation results before I fully commit."

Jeremy put his palm on her display-card and transferred a file with his engine specs and proposed flight. His equations filled the display. Alice entered a few commands and all of the equations changed.

"What did you do? None of it makes sense now." Jeremy scratched his temple as he scanned the newly formatted equations.

"I changed it to base twelve."

He raised his eyebrows. "Why did you do that?"

"It's a lot easier to work with the math. You should try it."

Jeremy shook his head. "I don't think so."

Ron shook his head too.

"This is interesting," Alice said. "I've never seen anything with these field patterns, and I've seen every engine spec that's ever been proposed to the corporation."

"If it was the same as everything else, it wouldn't get me out of point-debt."

"It'll never work for a Mars mission," she said.

Ron raised his chin. "That's what I said."

"It's only for near-body travel, like between the Earth and the Moon."

"These coefficients are wrong." She highlighted parts of several equations. "But it doesn't affect your overall propulsion vectors."

Jeremy was making a mental note to see exactly what she changed so he could update his spec.

"You could also fold this part of the equation into the performance vector." She entered more commands, and the equations moved around on the screen.

Jeremy's eyes widened. "That's not possible; you lose half of the computation."

She restored the equations and went through the process step by step. "If I factor out these components." She pointed at the display. "Then rearrange it so that the gravity vectors are balanced, the denominator goes to infinity and cancels out the rest." She continued to massage the equations and improve both their efficiency and validity.

Jeremy was both embarrassed by the adjustments to the equations he had spent years perfecting and also relieved that Alice didn't find any show-stoppers. By this point, he could no longer remember all of the changes she made and placed his palm back on the tabletop to retrieve the modifications. "Can you change it back to base ten before I make a copy?"

"Sure." She pressed a virtual button, and the screen full of equations converted back to what Jeremy understood.

"Do you think it can be done?" he asked.

"I believe it's possible," she replied.

"Round trip?"

Alice nodded.

"I appreciate your help. I've never actually seen you do your…thing." Jeremy waved his hand around.

"All I did was smooth out the wrinkles. You did all of the hard work."

"You're kind of amazing. Watching you do that is kind of surreal."

"You're starting to sound like everyone else," she said with a hint of disappointment.

"Sorry," Jeremy said. "We've got to leave, but I'll send you a message with details on when we're supposed to meet Theo." Excitement danced on his face.

"You said you were going to buy me a coffee," Ron interjected.

"We'll get you one to go." He got up from the table.

CHAPTER 9

THE PREP

After leaving the coffeehouse, Jeremy and Ron went to the Joint-Use Laboratory to prepare for Theo's meeting. It wasn't uncommon for indentured to be in the lab since many trainees—the ones with points—farmed out mundane tasks to them. Jeremy thought it was an unfair practice, but he didn't mind taking advantage of its acceptance so he and Ron could have a semi-private place to work.

The lab facility provided project teams with isolated cubicles to conduct research and perform testing. Each lab unit contained an interface to the corporate mainframe, several display-surfaces, and four chairs. A hundred lab units were available, but there were three times as many projects running. Also, the facility was only available from 8:00 a.m. to 8:00 p.m., making it a scarce and valuable trainee resource.

A frenzy of noobs trolled the facility for a cubicle to free up, but access was seniority based. If Jeremy had nothing else, he had an ample supply of credits, and he could always get a space. After identifying a new Mars project team, he not so politely told them that he was commandeering their lab. Arguing with seniority never proved point-positive at any level of the corporation, and the team left with no more resistance than an assortment of scowls. It wasn't a fair practice, but it was how the system worked. If Jeremy hadn't been displaced so many times during his earlier years, he would've already completed his project.

Once situated in the vacated cubicle, Jeremy synced the information in his embedded chip with the mainframe and showed Ron his updated design. "I hate to admit this, but Alice's tweaks added 5 percent thrust in the deflection manifold.

"Yeah, she's pretty awesome." Ron nodded. "I don't know why you go out of your way to avoid her. She's a genius. She's cute. She's point-positive. And she likes you."

"I don't have a problem with Alice. I just don't have time for something like that."

Ron grinned. "Like what...companionship? Romance? Love?"

"All wastes of time," Jeremy retorted. "None of them will help me become point-positive or get me out of my current situation."

"I hate to point this out," Rod said as he rubbed his brow. "But she just got you 5 percent more thrust in five minutes. Just think what you would get if she were around more."

"I don't deny that, but it's just not who I am. She just likes me because I don't gawk at her superpowers, and I even did that today."

"You can't be focused on your project so much that life passes you by or you're just a slave to the corporation, indentured or not."

Jeremy shook his head. "You have to look at the bigger picture. How do you think Alice's father would react if she brought home a point-sink like me?"

"He'll have a cow, for sure." Ron grinned.

"The Porchettas may not be super-rich like the Davenports, but they're many steps above me."

Ron waved his hand in a dismissive gesture. "Alice will outpace her father's career in no time if she hasn't already. She'll be able to do whatever she wants."

"He'll probably garnish her points," Jeremy said.

"It would've taken you hours on the AI mainframe to optimize your equations, and there's no guarantee that it would have made the same improvements. She did it while drinking coffee and simultaneously trying to get you to go on a date."

"I'm not disagreeing with you on what she's capable of."

"We don't know anything about her father, either. He might be a really nice guy."

Jeremy shook his head. "He's a mid-level exec. He's not a nice guy."

"Probably not, but we don't know that. We should give him the benefit of the doubt."

Jeremy brought up the fabrication model for his engine design on the lab unit's display. It showed a wireframe schematic of a ring. He adjusted the controls, and an animated representation, separated at a segment boundary, unrolled and divided up into forty individual, overlapping segments.

"Here's the rendering spec for the engine. There will be two identical rings composed of eighty individual segments."

Ron studied the diagram. "The trick is to fit your design into the unused space in the rendering plane. Think of it as fitting a square peg in a round hole. The Mars engine is the peg, and the rendering matrix is the hole. The peg is the largest square that will fit in the hole, and between each side of the peg and the hole, there is unused space. That's where we can render your engine."

Jeremy moved closer to the display. "And there'll be enough unused space?"

Ron did some computations on the lab terminal, and a diagram was displayed with the rendering area represented as a solid white circle. A black square grew from the center of the circle until it couldn't get any larger. "This is the current job." He dragged the representation of Jeremy's engine segments across the display with his finger and dropped them onto two of the unused areas around the square. He finessed the smaller segments until they fit into the unused space. "It'll take almost a full day to run, but it's doable."

"Can you generate a bill of materials?" Jeremy's palms were sweating.

Ron's fingers danced on the display's surface and a report appeared. "It'll take about a hundred kilos of stock, grade B filler and seventy-five kilos of grade A non-crystalline structural material."

"And?" Jeremy clenched his fists, waiting for the bad news.

"The largest requisition will be a hundred kilos of a class D, thermo-tolerant superconducting material."

Jeremy exhaled a long breath. "That's a lot."

"The non-superconductor materials are binding emulsifiers, so your engine will weigh just over a hundred kilos."

Jeremy looked at his display-card. "The design weight is a hundred and four kilos."

"It will take two consecutive shifts to complete all eighty segments."

"You've still got two unused areas around the Mars segment. Just use them all and cut the time in half."

"I can't use the top or front sides because it would be obvious to anyone walking by that I wasn't making a Mars engine."

Jeremy nodded conceding to Ron's expertise. "How are you going to manage two consecutive shifts?"

"I'm sure I can make a deal with the night tech to take over her shift, but you're going to have to get the contraband out of there on your own. I'll have to finish the Mars run. I'm also going to need some stims because I'll have to make it through the next shift too."

Jeremy shifted in his chair. "Are you sure you can make it thirty-six hours straight?"

"I'll manage, but I'll need the stims. I'm more worried about you getting your segments out of the facility without getting caught."

"I have a plan." Jeremy smiled. "The maintenance shaft I used this morning will provide a discreet way out of the facility, but I'm going to have to find someone to help."

CHAPTER 10

THE APPOINTMENT

The next morning, Jeremy was already awake when the lights came on and the bell rang at 5:00 a.m. He was polishing up his presentation, again. He wanted it to be as convincing as possible so Theo wouldn't renege on his offer. Jeremy was also enjoying the satisfaction of encapsulating his whole project into a single cohesive presentation.

Alice's suggestions simplified some of the more complex mathematical aspects of Jeremy's design, and that made a much cleaner run through of the near-body propulsion theories. Jeremy understood the formulas backward and forward but explaining them to others had always been a challenge. Alice had made that job easier.

Jeremy wondered why he hadn't paid much attention to Alice's abilities in the past. If they ended up going on a date, he would have an opportunity to see what else she could do. Except, his complete disinterest in her talents was the main reason she liked him. Jeremy frowned. The seconds he wasted thinking about Alice reminded him that relationships were too much of a distraction, and he went back to working on his presentation.

Jeremy waited until the clock on his display-card showed exactly 8:02 a.m. He didn't want to appear too anxious for the call, but he wanted to get the meeting set up and the call over with. He brought up the contact information Theo had provided at The Launch Pad and pulled a pair of earbuds out of his pocket. He popped the archaic devices into his ears while wishing he had implants, but they were high-point mods he couldn't justify. His display-card showed a virtual representation of an old-fashioned business card that was probably only good for one use. He hoped Theo would answer when he clicked the link to initiate the call because he didn't want to leave a message. After a seemingly long wait, the connection status turned green, and a female voice began speaking.

"Hello, Mr. Scott. My name is Monica, and I'll be helping you schedule with Mr. Davenport."

"Thank you," he said. "How did you know who I was?"

"Mr. Davenport assigned this link to you, and I was expecting your call."

"I thought I would be talking to Theo. Is he available?"

"I schedule all of Mr. Davenport's activities, and I've tentatively penciled you in for tomorrow afternoon at three thirty."

"It will have to be after six o'clock. Two of my associates will be joining me for the meeting, and they won't be able to meet that early in the day."

"Ah, yes. Miss Porchetta and Mr. Newcomb."

Jeremy didn't know how she knew that, but he suspected Theo had been spying on his activities. "They're an important part of the project and really need to be at the meeting."

"All right, I was able to shuffle Mr. Davenport's schedule, and he'll be available at seven thirty tomorrow evening."

"Where's the meeting?"

"A private pod will be sent for you. Be ready to depart at seven o'clock in the Davenport's private terminal suite. The necessary passes will be sent to you and your guests momentarily."

"Where's the private terminal?"

"I'm sending you a full itinerary right now with directions. If you have any questions, please reply to the message."

"Thanks." He heard a chime in his ear indicating the receipt of the information."

"Goodbye," she said and ended the call.

Jeremy quickly skimmed through the itinerary he received from Monica. He, Alice, and Ron were going to be guests at the Davenport estate.

Monica, he thought, was a bot. An impressive bot but nevertheless a bot. It annoyed Jeremy that someone as rich as Theo would spend points on a fancy computer program pretending to be a human instead of paying an actual person who needed the points. Theo was an asshole. Everything Jeremy had preconceived about him was apparently true, but at least he had made it to the next step.

CHAPTER 11

THE FAUX EQUATIONS

Jeremy sent Alice a message to see if she could meet up before Ron finished his shift. He wanted to practice his presentation before a live audience, and he believed she would be honest with him about the content before he actually showed it to Theo. Alice responded that she would be at the coffeehouse after 5:00 p.m.

Jeremy spent the rest of the morning and all afternoon in the Joint-Use Lab working on his project. There were still items on his checklist to complete. If Theo provided the raw materials to build the engine, he needed to be ready. Also, being occupied with work prevented him from dwelling on his problems.

After a productive day, Jeremy left for the coffeehouse. He got there early, and most of the tables were empty. The coffeehouse was open most of the day, but until first shift was over, it had little traffic. He got the same table they sat at the previous day. He placed his palm on the table to bring up the menu and scrolled through the options. He preferred a beer, but he selected a black coffee and ordered it. Real coffee no longer existed, but the synthetic replacement was good enough. Jeremy's generation had never experienced actual coffee, so he didn't know the difference anyway.

Alice walked in the door at 5:05 p.m. She worked at the Theoretical Sciences Facility, and the coffeehouse was on the way to her corporate apartment. She saw Jeremy as soon as she entered and went straight over to him.

"Are you ready?" she asked.

Jeremy sat his coffee down on the table. "I'm probably as ready as I'll ever be, but I wanted to run through it with you and see what you thought."

"Let's see what you've got." She pulled out a chair and sat down.

"My presentation's only thirty minutes, but I've tried to research every possible question Theo could ask and have data to back up my response."

"It'll be best to keep it all high level. All of his questions are going to be point-based, not technical."

"I'm ready for that. I made sure to have all the figures needed to compute the point-per-kilogram cost of ferrying cargo to and from the Moon, and what the breakdown is. I've also got the new simulation results for the spacecraft after being modified for the round trip and using your updates to the field equations."

"Okay, dazzle me." She smiled and leaned back in her chair. The server brought her a cappuccino that she hadn't even ordered. When he sat it down, she smiled her thanks.

Jeremy used the table's built-in display to present his pitch. It took about thirty minutes, as he predicted, and he had dumbed-down the technical aspects as much as he could without losing the crux of his design.

"I think your presentation is excellent." Alice made a small frown. "But you're giving away too much information."

"If I don't provide the details, I can't prove it'll work."

"I've said this before, but I'll say it again. You can't trust Theo. He'll take those equations and reverse engineer your whole design."

Jeremy laughed. "He's not smart enough to do that."

Alice lifted a single eyebrow. "But he's smart enough to hire someone to do it for him."

Jeremy shook his head. "If he's going to fund my project for credit, why would he try that?"

"If he reverse engineers your design, he'll get all the credit."

"Nobody trusts Theo less than I do, but I'm desperate here, and I've got to assume he's being legit for this to work."

"That's precisely the problem. You're desperate, and he knows it. But he's also desperate, and he'll have no qualms about using you to get what he really wants."

"Are you saying that I shouldn't show him the presentation?" Jeremy raised his eyebrows.

"No, you should still give the presentation. Use all of your cost-benefit analysis and other non-technical details, but we're going to make some modifications to your field equations."

Jeremy lowered his chin. "I don't have time to do that and make them look legitimate."

Alice smiled. "I can." She used her finger to pull up the equations on the display and then tweaked, reordered, and massaged the numbers and symbols so they still looked like a valid set of equations. "These will yield the expected values for a small range of inputs, but the fundamental parts of your theory have been completely factored out."

Jeremy's eyes widened. "It would take me a while to figure out these weren't the real equations, and I would need time on the simulator to know for sure."

"That's that idea." She smiled again.

"Why are you so suspicious of Theo?"

"I don't believe the Davenports got to their position in life through charity and goodwill to others."

"I don't either, but Theo's got the points to throw around, and I might as well benefit from them."

"You also shouldn't bring the real equations with you. That private train is probably filled with sniffers."

Jeremy jerked his head back. "Just how well do you know Theo?"

"I know him well enough to be cautious."

Jeremy snorted. "It just seems crazy to fake my presentation when I have a legitimate project."

The two updated the presentation to use the faux equations and purged the internal storage of Jeremy's embedded chip so it contained only the modified version. He hoped Alice was wrong about Theo, or he was screwed.

CHAPTER 12

THE CHECKLIST

Alice and Jeremy left the coffeehouse in time to meet Ron outside the Large-Scale Fabrication Facility. Ron was the first one to exit the building when first shift ended. He waved as soon as he saw them.

"I thought we were supposed to meet at the terminal," he said.

"You were on our way from the coffeehouse," Jeremy said.

"I discussed taking over second shift with my counterpart. She seemed okay with it."

"Did you tell her what you were going to do?" Jeremy asked.

Ron shook his head. "She'll need plausible deniability if everything goes south."

Jeremy narrowed his eyes. "Also, Alice doesn't trust Theo, and this may all be for nothing."

"I didn't say that," she countered. "I said you needed to take precautions, and you did."

"I'm going to be in a disastrous situation if this doesn't pan out." Jeremy ran his fingers through his hair and imagined how he'd look as a bald dent.

"Did you come up with something to give Theo credit for?" Ron asked.

"Patron," Jeremy said.

"That may be accurate," Alice said, "but it's not technical."

"Logistics coordinator?" Jeremy asked.

"It's got to have a point-bias," she said.

"Mining development," Jeremy said. "No…how about near-body mining development?"

"Near-body, extra-terrestrial mining development and logistics," Alice said.

Ron laughed. "That's a mouthful."

"It might be pompous enough to match his ego," Jeremy said.

It was a twenty-minute walk to the terminal from the fabrication facility, so the three headed in that direction.

"Have you two been on a tube-train before?" Ron asked.

Jeremy shook his head. "Have you?"

"When I checked into the Resource Distribution Center on the west coast. They packed as many of us as they could fit into a cargo pod with no seats, and we spent the next forty-eight hours traveling here. We made at least a hundred stops, but we couldn't get out of the pod."

"Corporate spared no expense," Jeremy said sarcastically.

"They also used mid-grade gravity deflectors in the cargo pod's drive assembly, and every time we accelerated the uneven field flow set off a chain-reaction of pukers."

Jeremy wrinkled up his face at the thought of it.

"I assure you that Theo's pod will not be like that," Alice said. "It'll be luxurious."

"Are you speaking from experience?" Jeremy didn't think Alice and Theo had much in common, but maybe he didn't know everything.

"I know how people like the Davenports operate, and that pod is the gateway to their estate. It'll be fabulous." She raised her hands and stretched out her fingers.

"So, what's it like to ride on a tube-train?" Jeremy asked.

"I just told you. It's awful," Ron said.

"How did you get to the campus?" Alice asked.

"I was born here," Jeremy said.

"You've never left the campus?" She knew it took points to travel, but she thought everyone had been somewhere.

"I've been to the launch facility a few times. It's nine hundred kilometers southeast of the campus."

"How did you get there?" she asked.

"A hover-type, cargo drone makes a plodding journey about three meters off the ground. There's no passenger compartment, so you have to hang out in the hold for eighteen hours."

"That doesn't sound like much fun," Alice said.

"It wasn't bad. It was sort of relaxing."

"It sounds a lot better than my train ride," Ron said, and all three laughed.

"How are you going to get your spacecraft launched when everyone knows your project was canceled?" Alice asked.

"I was given a week to wrap up, and nobody said I couldn't do my scheduled tests."

"Aren't they going to know something's up and ask you what you're doing?"

Jeremy shook his head. "Nobody's going to ask about my project. If they do, I'll start asking about their project, and they'll leave for sure. It's too competitive to share project info."

Alice's eyes narrowed. "Wouldn't you all get more accomplished if you worked together?"

"That's not how it works." Jeremy laughed. "The corporation believes that competition makes trainees work harder."

"It's not that way in Theoretical Sciences," she said.

"That's because you're not competing for employment. You got to skip all of this because you're smarter than everyone else." Jeremy was surprised she was so oblivious to how the trainee program worked.

"I still don't understand how that's going to keep anyone from interfering."

Jeremy sighed. "As the story goes, a trainee once had a conversation with another trainee in a different project team. They talked about the details of their projects. Later on, there were multiple claims on the intellectual property, some violence ensued, and the corporation retired everyone involved. True or not, nobody's going to risk that by discussing their project with another team member."

"It's totally different in my department. It's all about collaboration and helping each other," Alice said.

"How much do they help you?" Jeremy asked.

Alice didn't respond. She had never thought about that before.

Jeremy saw the public terminal ahead of them. "Are you having second thoughts? Either of you?"

"I'm in all the way," Ron said without hesitation.

"I'm not having second thoughts. I just want your project to succeed," she said. "And that means precautions have to be taken."

The three approached the steps that led down to the public terminal.

CHAPTER 13

THE TERMINAL

There were no personal vehicles on the corporate campus. Only the extraordinarily wealthy could afford such luxury, and none of them had any desire to go anywhere on their own. Automobiles were odd, inefficient contraptions in old vids. Creating and maintaining roads and highways was deemed too inefficient and expensive for corporate logistics, so transportation was reimagined. Communities organized around their sponsor corporation, and everything an employee needed could be reached by walking. There were automated shuttle services available to ferry employees within a corporate campus, but that was also a luxury and only used for special occasions, such as an executive-level promotion or to parade a high-ranking corporate officer in front of the plebes.

Transportation for intercampus travel was handled by tubular trains, and they could get you anywhere in the world that had a corporate presence. Tube-trains, as they were called, were an extension of an early twenty-first-century technology that propelled small pods through tubes buried in the ground. Once this technology took hold, it quickly replaced all automobiles, planes, boats, and conventional trains.

Theo lived over four hundred kilometers from the corporate campus at his family's estate. It was a fortified compound of pure opulence and safely removed from the throngs of commoners. It might seem that such a distance from the campus would create an unfathomable daily commute, but the Davenports had a private tube line that travelled nonstop to the campus at over 1,600 KPH. Theo's commute was less than twenty luxurious minutes, a lot less time than it took most trainees to walk from their barracks to their first seminar.

Tube-trains used gravity deflection to levitate and propel the transport pods through a network of tubes kept at a near vacuum. The airtight pods required a seal to be formed between them and the gates after arriving at the terminal. The gate would open like elevator doors and allow its occupants to enter or leave without losing any of the tube's vacuum. The transport system was fast, safe, and effective. It also had more in common with the Mars missions than it did with any conventional trains from the past.

The public terminal was located at the center of the corporate campus. It looked like a giant hole in the ground with concentric circles forming steps. Jeremy, Alice, and Ron descended the steps twenty meters below the surface and entered a doorway cut into a section of the bottom steps. The terminal itself was fifty meters long, five meters wide, and completely devoid of architectural style. Its white walls were brightly lit, and there were no embellishments of any kind beyond the black borders around the pod gates and their identifying numbers. The terminal was empty except for one executive waiting in front of the fifth gate halfway down and a couple of cleaning drones meandering around in algorithmic patterns.

The three walked the length of the terminal past all ten gates. Ron nodded hello to the waiting executive, but he only eyed them with suspicion as they passed by. When they reached the end, there was an opaque glass door. Few employees, and even fewer trainees, had ever ventured beyond this point.

Jeremy put his palm flat on the door's surface and a green light illuminated around his hand. The door silently retracted into the wall after he removed his hand. Two corporate security officers were on the other side, but they didn't say anything as the three entered the restricted area. There were ten more doors lining the corridor. Each one led to a private waiting room and gate. According to the itinerary, the Davenport's was the last one. Jeremy put his palm flat on the waiting room door, but nothing happened.

"Why isn't it letting us in?" Jeremy asked.

"We're a few minutes early," Ron said. "Maybe it has to be seven o'clock before we can enter."

"We got through the first door," Jeremy said.

"Try it again," Alice said.

Jeremy placed his hand back on the glass surface, but nothing happened.

"One more time," she said.

Jeremy tried a third time, and a green outline appeared. "It worked. How'd you know?"

"It's an old trick to put people in their place. I would bet anyone who isn't a Davenport gets denied on their first try."

The door opened when Jeremy removed his hand, and two more corporate security guards were waiting for them. It was just a foyer with barely enough room for the two muscular men. Behind them was a pair of double doors each made of carved wood and embellished with an excessive amount of gold leaf.

"You're early," one of the guards said.

"Maybe five minutes," Jeremy said.

"Were you sent an itinerary?" he said in a condescending tone.

"Yes, it said to be here at seven o'clock."

"It's not seven o'clock."

"Were we supposed to wait outside the door?" Jeremy raised his eyebrows.

"You should have followed the itinerary." The guard stared down at him with cold eyes.

The second guard walked over to Jeremy and held out a large display-card. It showed his ID photo at the top corner and an outline for his hand. Jeremy placed his hand on the surface and confirmed his identity.

"Miss Porchetta," the guard said and held the device out for her. It showed her picture at the top, and she complied with the scanning of her implanted chip.

"Aren't you going to verify Ron?" Jeremy asked after the guards made no effort to scan him.

"No dents allowed in the pod," the second guard said. Ron was wearing his solid gray work uniform, which clearly denoted his position—as did his mandatory shaven head.

"He has an invitation," Jeremy said.

"We only have passes for a Jeremy Scott and an Alice Porchetta."

"Then you're wrong." Jeremy snorted. "You should also have one for a Ron Newcomb. Check again."

"Dents aren't allowed," the guard repeated as he shook his head.

"It's not a big deal," Ron said. "I can wait here until you get back."

"You're part of the team, and you have an invitation. You're going, or none of us are." Jeremy wasn't sure he really meant what he said, but he hoped the guards got the message.

"Don't risk your project just to get me on the train," Ron said. "It's not worth it."

Jeremy pulled out a small display-card from his pocket and proceeded to send a message to Monica-bot saying that she must have a glitch in her programming because she didn't get the appropriate pass sent for Ron, and the three of them would be waiting at the terminal until the matter was resolved. It was a gamble, but Jeremy thought it was worth a try.

A few seconds later, the guard's display-card chimed, and a picture of Ron appeared at the top of it.

Jeremy crossed his arms. "I told you he had a pass."

The guard scanned Ron and put the display-card away. The wooden doors opened inward to reveal the waiting room. It was gaudy and baroque to the extreme. It looked like the palace of a spoiled king. A ten-meter cube was covered from top to bottom in flocked wallpaper. A crystal chandelier hung from the ceiling, and thick rugs covered the floor. Classic paintings hung on one wall like a museum exposition, complete with gallery lighting and velvet ropes to keep onlookers at bay. The gate was the centerpiece, and it was surrounded by a plush burgundy theater curtain topped with a heavily bunted valance. The gate itself, in the center, looked like a classic painting from a master depicting angels and overweight men and women, all naked. Jeremy and Ron both stared slack-jawed at the spectacle.

"It's a hologram," Alice said, trying to counteract their overwhelmed state.

"How do you know?" Jeremy asked. "It's flawless."

Ron was speechless.

"The curtains around the gate are probably real as are the ropes in front of the Rembrandt and Van Gogh paintings, but look carefully at the walls." She pointed to a specific area.

"If it's a hologram, I don't see anything to indicate it." Jeremy walked over to the paintings for a closer inspection.

"You can just make out the fractal patterns used to create the illusion. It repeats throughout the image, and it's not natural."

Jeremy shook his head. "I don't see any patterns."

"They're there," she said. "If they had hired an actual holo-artist instead of using an AI to create the image, you wouldn't have been able to tell."

The guards closed the doors behind them, and the three could hear a pod arriving behind the gate. The mechanical articulations of the seal could be heard as well as an assortment of hissing and crinkling sounds as the coupling of the pod to the gate completed.

The gate doors pulled apart and broke the illusion of the painting as the two sides retracted into the wall. There was a slight rush of air over their faces, followed by the delicate scent of flowers and nature rushing out of the pod.

"What drama queens," Alice said.

"It's fantastic," Ron finally said after regaining his ability to speak.

"All that glitters isn't gold," she warned.

CHAPTER 14

THE POD

The Davenport's pod was not as outlandish as the waiting room. It was extremely nice but more executive-chic than palatial-rococo. The tube lines were three meters in diameter, and the pods were slightly smaller. All private pods were different, depending on their owner's taste, point reserves, and desire to impress others. Some were functional, like a mobile office, and others were pure luxury. The Davenport's pod was somewhere between the two extremes, but it definitely leaned toward the luxury end of the spectrum.

The inside perimeter was lined with a leather sofa all the way around the pod except for the gate opening. A small, round table was situated at each end of the pod's capsule-shaped floor plan. A delicate arrangement of flowers in a tall crystal vase floated a couple of centimeters above each table's surface, obviously a hologram. A carved wooden console in the center of the pod provided a fully-stocked bar with at least a hundred bottles of liquor, some over a hundred years old. Trays of delicate pastries and fresh fruit were also provided. Jeremy and Ron had never seen actual fruit before. The pod walls were concave as they went from floor to ceiling, but they appeared as unobstructed windows looking out in all directions. The view was from ten meters above the ground looking at the concentric circle steps leading down to the terminal. In reality, the pod had no actual windows, was sealed in a vacuum-tight tube, and was twenty meters below ground, so the scenery was either a simulation or a live view.

Jeremy, Alice, and Ron entered the pod and sat around one of the tables. They couldn't tell if it was the front or the back of the pod since it was symmetric. A chime sounded three times, and the gate closed. A hissing sound could be heard as the pod separated itself from the seal and there was a slight bump as the gravity deflectors engaged. Jeremy's ears popped as the pod adjusted its internal pressure, and they started to move.

The pod's propulsion system minimized the sensation of motion. Rings, similar to the Mars engines, were circumscribed inside of the cylinder portion of the pod's capsule-shaped body. One ring was situated at each end of the pod's length and another in the center. They created a gravity cushion around the pod so it wouldn't come in contact with the tube wall and propelled it up to 2,000 KPH. The rings were also able to cancel out a great deal of the inertia generated as the pod accelerated to cruising speed. Only the view out the virtual windows gave any indication of how fast the pod was actually traveling, and the elevated viewpoint kept the eyes and inner ear synchronized to prevent motion sickness.

Ten minutes into the seventeen-minute trip, Jeremy's display-card notified him of an attempted hack into his embedded chip. He had set up a monitoring routine after Alice warned him about Theo just to see if he would actually try anything. Jeremy then received a message on his display-card saying the meeting had been canceled. The pod slowed to a stop and reversed its direction.

"Damn it," Jeremy yelled. "He just downloaded all of the project data including my presentation."

"I warned you not to trust him," Alice said and cocked her head to the side.

"He'll learn soon enough that he stole bogus information." Jeremy addressed the empty portion of the pod, figuring Theo was eavesdropping on them. "If you really want to get that credit you need so badly, then you're going to have to do better than this. Now I understand why you can't get promoted."

Alice put her hand on Jeremy's shoulder to help calm him down, but it was too late.

CHAPTER 15

THE SAVE

"How's he able to steal information out of my chipset?" Jeremy asked. "That's supposed to be impossible."

"We don't know that's what he did," Ron said.

"That's exactly what he did," Alice said. "It's a common ploy with the Davenports."

"How do you know that?" Jeremy asked.

"My family has dealt with the Davenports before. Any offer for a ride on their private tube-line is a setup for something."

"Even if he only got the spoofed equations, I'm not going to get the funding for the project. I still lose."

"You're overlooking your biggest advantage in this situation." Alice smiled. "The worst thing that can happen to you is that you'll drop one rung on the corporate ladder. Theo's fall will be so far, he'll break his neck. He's much more desperate for this project to succeed than you are."

"If he's not going to get us the raw materials, I've lost. It doesn't matter how desperate he is."

"You haven't lost yet." She pulled a small object out of her pocket. It was a black cube with no markings or any other indication of what its function was.

"What's that?" Ron stared at the mysterious item.

"This is a monitoring cube." She held it up between her thumb and index finger. "It uses quantum encryption to store all of the changes in the electromagnetic spectrum within a three-meter radius. It also logs its exact spatial co-ordinate."

Jeremy's face tightened. "How is that going to help me?"

"Any in-depth chipset scan has a specific electromagnetic signature. It's unmistakable. When that's followed by bulk data transfer and paired with our location inside the Davenport's private tube-line kilometers from the campus, we have infallible proof that your information was stolen via a means prohibited by corporate protocol." Alice smirked. "This evidence could be devastating if it were to somehow get into the hands of the right person. Not just for Theo, either."

"He's just going to say we made the whole thing up or fabricated the evidence," Jeremy said.

"I'm sure he'll try that, but the cube's data is irrefutable. There's no way to tamper with it without detection."

The pod slowed to a stop, and the virtual view outside the pod was replaced with an oversized image of Theo sitting behind a large, ornate desk in an executive chair with an outlandish back that rose half a meter above his head. Jeremy thought he looked like a child sitting in an oversized chair.

"It looks as though we have a little problem," Theo scoffed.

"You tried to steal my engine," Jeremy yelled at the screen.

"I was simply verifying its authenticity. Did you think I was going to invest a hundred thousand points without some confidence it's going to be successful?"

Jeremy clenched his fists. "You could have waited to see my presentation before making that decision."

"Instead of using technology banned by the corporation," Alice added.

"Hi, Alice." Theo smirked. "I should have known you would've calculated some scheme to blackmail me."

"This isn't blackmail. I'm just making sure you do what you said. So far, you aren't doing a very good job of it."

Theo sighed. "I'm the one who is putting up the points. I have a responsibility to myself to make sure this is a legitimate venture."

"I'm sure everyone will believe that," she said sarcastically.

Theo's nostrils flared. "You still have to get out of the pod. I can simply have the security guards at the gate remove the cube from you."

"I'll transmit the data if I think there's any danger of that."

Theo grinned. "But you won't be able to use the quantum verification if you transmit the data."

"It'll be enough to get someone to question the technological content of this pod, and I'm sure all of those who've ridden in here will go back and see if any of their information has ever mysteriously turned up in Davenport hands."

Theo leaned in closer to the camera, and his face filled the entire wall of the pod. "What do you want?"

"Fund the project," she said. "That's what you said you would do in the first place. I've already validated the engine design. It's legitimate."

Theo leaned back in his chair and crossed his arms. "I'm not going to give you any points."

"I just need the material requisitions," Jeremy said.

Theo pushed his chair away from the desk and stood. "If this project fails, you'll all be in serious trouble."

"Instead of threatening us, you should try helping us," Jeremy said.

"I'll get you an acquisition code tomorrow morning. Material supply is fungible, and I'll only offset the amount you've specified. If you use more than you've specified, it will be on you."

"The authorization has to be available when my shift starts at six o'clock," Ron said.

"It'll be there." Theo sneered before the pod's walls returned to their simulated view of the outside.

CHAPTER 16

THE LICORICE

The pod started moving again, but it was headed back to the campus. The meeting was over. When the pod doors opened, the two guards came forward to escort Jeremy, Alice, and Ron out of the waiting room.

The three left the public terminal as quickly as they could. They didn't want to have any problems with corporate security, who would certainly be loyal to Theo, or at least to his father. They ascended the concentric steps two at a time and headed down the main corridor through the campus.

Once they were a couple of blocks away, Jeremy turned to Alice. "What the fuck just happened?"

"I told you that Theo couldn't be trusted."

Jeremy's brow furrowed. "And you brought in some espionage technology to blackmail him?"

She pulled out the black cube and held it up between her fingers. Then she plopped it in her mouth and started chewing. "Licorice." She held her hand in front of her mouth as she spoke.

"You bluffed Theo with a piece of candy?" Jeremy said in an incredulous tone.

Alice smirked. "It got you the raw materials didn't it?"

"I guess we're going to have to wait until tomorrow morning to find out."

"What are we going to do when it comes time to fork over the cube?"

"By then, you'll have hopefully sent and returned the spacecraft, and he won't care that I made it up. He may eventually be able to figure out that I was fibbing from the pod's sensor logs."

"How do you know so much about Theo?"

Alice looked down at the ground. "I didn't want to bring this up…but we sort of dated for about three months during my first year here."

Ron's eyes widened. "No way."

"At the time, he was obsessed with me."

"Sexually or mathematically?" Jeremy asked.

"Neither," she said. "He just wanted to parade me around his inner circle of friends and show off my parlor tricks."

"And you're just now bringing this up?" Jeremy mouth turned into a slight frown.

"It's embarrassing. I was his shiny new thing until I had performed in front of everyone he wanted to impress. Then he moved on to the next shiny thing. I didn't know what kind of person he was back then."

Jeremy stopped walking. "How did you know about the data scrapper in the pod?"

Alice faced Jeremy. "When we dated, Theo started showing up unexpectedly beyond any reasonable statistical probability. He knew where I was going to be and knew more than he should have about my friends and colleagues. I correlated all of his coincidental activities with the information in my private schedule and estimated an 89 percent chance that there was some form of data pilfering going on in relationship to my ride in the pod."

"You probably should have told us that."

"Would you enjoy telling people you dated Theo?"

Jeremy shook his head.

"And I brought a bag of licorice to use in case of an emergency."

"I guess it's a good thing you did. Faking the equations was a good idea too."

"Like I said, you can't trust Theo."

"I know. I know." Jeremy smiled. "Is there such a thing as a monitoring cube?"

"There is," she said. "I've worked on them, and they do look just like a piece of candy."

"I guess we'll find out in the morning if the mission's a go," Jeremy said.

Ron's lips parted before he spoke. "What's licorice?"

Alice pulled out a small wax paper bag from her pocket and handed it to Ron.

CHAPTER 17

THE FABRICATION

The next morning, Ron was early for work and relieved the second shift operator a few minutes before first shift started. Jeremy snuck back into the Large-Scale Fabrication Facility through the maintenance shaft and met Ron at his fabricator.

"Theo sent the authorization code this morning. Are you ready to give it a try?" Jeremy asked.

Ron sat on the edge of his chair. "Let's do it." He entered the code Jeremy showed him. It took a few seconds for anything to happen, but then a graphical display of the inventory levels increased for several items. "The system accepted the code."

Both of them exhaled with relief.

"Here's the final fabrication plan." Jeremy placed his palm on the console to transfer the information.

Ron prepped the data and inlaid the design into the hidden sections of the rendering plane. "If the raw materials are really available, the pre-check won't complain about the increased material requirements. This is the real test." He continued entering commands on the console. A series of red lights in the virtual controls turned green, one after another. The last red light took longer than the others, but it finally changed.

"Does that mean it's going to run?" Jeremy asked.

Ron smiled. "We're good to go."

Jeremy's posture relaxed by a small degree. "Are you going to be able to work thirty-six hours straight?"

"If you got the stims, I'll be able to make it. I also added two dozen alarms to notify me with a loud tone if anything even looks like it's about to go wrong."

"I would offer to help you, but I don't know if I could actually contribute."

"Your engine segments won't be accessible until a Mars engine segment completes. When I clear the rack, you'll have to get your stuff out of there, and I won't be able to help. Then you're going to have to get your segments out of the facility, and I can't help with that either."

Jeremy sighed. "I'm working on that part of the plan."

"I'm going to start the renderer." Ron looked at Jeremy for confirmation before entering the start-up sequence.

Jeremy nodded.

The fabricator started making noise as the material feeds primed and the renderer was purged with a blast of high-pressure nitrogen. It made a plume of condensate from the chamber housing all the way to the ceiling. A faint popping sounded a few times per second as the fabricator started out-putting one molecular layer at a time. The frequency ramped up until it was a high-pitched tone.

"Now the fun part." Jeremy frowned. "Waiting."

"You've got two hours until the first batch is ready. You need to have your plan in place to get them out of here by then."

"I will," Jeremy said. "I hope."

CHAPTER 18

THE SEGMENTS

A Mars engine was composed of 360 individual segments. One for each degree of the ring, and each one measured approximately eighty-seven centimeters long. The ends of each segment were slightly angled creating a trapezoidal prism shape. When joined end-to-end, they created the ring's circular shape. It took thirty days—or 720 hours—of fabrication to complete a ten-meter ring.

The lunar engine segments were only sixteen centimeters long and weighed only 1,300 grams. There was one segment for every eighteen degrees of the one-meter ring, but they overlapped in an offset manor like two rows of bricks in a wall. This overlapping design required twice as many segments for the same linear length, but it was a unique characteristic of the near-body propulsion engine. Each segment was also slightly curved to create a perfectly circular ring when assembled.

A large-scale fabricator produced one segment of a Mars engine ring every two hours, including the time it took to unload the segment from the extruder, inspect it, and load it onto an automated drone-cart using a robotic manipulator arm. As soon as the segment was loaded, the cart would whisk the segment away to a staging area. The fabrication of the next segment would start immediately.

Seven lunar segments could be created alongside each Mars segment. Every two hours, Jeremy would need to smuggle a new batch out of the facility to his staging area. He knew he could hide them, two at a time, in the pockets of his uniform and carry them down the central corridor to the maintenance shaft. He did not, however, believe it would be possible to make forty roundtrips past fourteen fabricators and not draw any attention.

Not only would it be odd for Jeremy to pass by the fabricators that many times, a project manager, like himself, shouldn't be in the fabrication facility in the first place. The blue shirt under his overalls would draw attention like a flashing holographic sign. Even if he changed up his route, there weren't enough permutations to avoid passing by the same fabricator multiple times. He considered borrowing Ron's gray shirt to blend in better, but his hair would give him away and dents weren't allowed to roam the corridors either.

Corporate security also patrolled the facility every hour. Jeremy believed he could bluff his way out of one or two encounters, but timing would be critical. Too many confrontations with them would be disastrous to his plan.

If Jeremy could reach the maintenance shaft without detection, he could openly carry the segments without drawing much attention since he would be back in his own domain.

While it would be easy once he got the segments out of the Large-Scale Fabrication Facility, he was going to have to come up with a better plan than carrying them by hand.

CHAPTER 19

THE DRONE PARADE

Operators were perched high above the facility's floor on a platform affixed to the top of their fabricators. Pipes and control panels blocked most of their lateral views, but grated floor panels made it possible to see the main corridor below, and that was a potential problem for Jeremy's plan to smuggle his lunar segments out of the facility.

After surveying the area from atop Ron's fabricator, Jeremy noticed the stream of supply-drones running along each side of the main corridor in cordoned-off areas next to the fabricators. The drones were a half-meter long, six-wheeled, and each carried a payload of raw materials. An AI managed requests from all of the active jobs and sent a supply-drone to the appropriate store, retrieved a payload module, and delivered it to a fabricator.

The payloads could be any of the raw materials used by the fabricators ranging from a super-conducting suspension to a basic element like iron dust or liquid helium. The modules were sealed containers with identification chips, and there was no visible indication of their contents.

The drones were mostly hidden from anyone walking down the corridor between the fabricators, and that gave Jeremy an idea. "How closely are those supply-drones monitored?"

"It's a fully automated system, no human intervention. But the inventory AI would certainly detect any tampering," Ron said.

"I don't see any cameras, but I guess there are proximity sensors of some sort to keep them from running into each other."

"I've seen them run into operators where they cross to the other side of the corridor, so they must not have much in terms of sensors, just location transponders."

"What happened when they ran into someone?"

"All of the drones stopped."

"Do they start back up?"

"Most of the time. One had to be lifted off the operator, and it set off an alarm."

"They probably scaled back the sensor packs to cut costs."

"Probably," Ron said. "Only indentured work here, so they aren't too concerned about safety."

Jeremy rubbed his chin. "What's their route?"

Ron pointed down the corridor. "They leave the supply store, go down the other side of the corridor, cross over, then down this side before returning to the supply store."

"If I set an engine segment on top of a drone, it would ride all the way to the end of the corridor. Nobody would see it."

"Maybe." Ron was visualizing the path to see if Jeremy's plan would actually work. "It would have to be an empty drone or you'll lose the segment inside a fabricator when it unloads."

"I can work with that." Jeremy was pleased with the irony of his scheme. The corporation put the supply drones in place to eliminate the possibility of someone stealing raw materials, but it was the perfect tool for smuggling his engine segments out of the facility. He grinned widely. "I've got a plan. I just have to recruit some more help to make it work."

Jeremy anxiously waited two hours for the first batch of lunar segments to emerge from the fabricator. He had to crouch down and be quiet while the fabrication commenced. He didn't want to distract Ron, nor did he want to attract any undue attention. It was a long two hours, but Jeremy worked on his proposed flight plan while he waited.

"First batch is up." Ron directed a robotic manipulator arm to move into position. "You've got to get your pieces off the extrusion racks as soon as the Mars segment is clear. I have to start the next job as soon as I can."

"I'm ready." Jeremy took a deep breath and climbed up on the racks.

The mechanical arm had ten joints and moved more like a tentacle than a human appendage. It had a monstrous hand at its end with ten pairs of opposing fingers to delicately grip the Mars segment with polydactyl articulation.

After the arm transferred the Mars segment to a drone-cart, Jeremy offloaded the seven curved bricks that were left behind. He slid two segments into the large pockets in the front of his overalls and lined the rest up under the racks to get them out of sight. The hidden cargo in his pockets made him look a lot heavier, but even with point-allocated nutrition, there were overweight trainees. Besides, he couldn't be seen toting around bricks made of superconducting material in a place he didn't belong. "I'll be back."

Ron glanced back at him. "Don't get caught."

Jeremy nodded and leaned over the edge of the elevated platform to see if the corridor was clear. He proceeded down the ladder and headed to the maintenance shaft. He was almost there when a corporate security officer rounded the corner and almost ran into him.

"What's a project specialist doing in this facility?" the guard asked, staring down at Jeremy.

Jeremy's insides trembled, but he knew a confrontation like this was a possibility and had already planned how he was going to bluff his way through it. "I came to see what the fuck was taking my job so long," he said with as hostile a tone as he thought he could get away with.

"Do you have authorization to be here?" the man asked.

"Do you have authorization to delay my project? Do you know how many points you're costing me? Who's your manager? I'm going to have your points docked by whatever it's costing me." Jeremy's nostrils flared. He had no such authority to dock anyone's points, but he hoped the officer wouldn't realize that.

"There are strict corporate guidelines."

"Guidelines?" Jeremy said in a sharp tone. "That's all they are. If you'll excuse me, I'll be on my way unless you want to waste even more points." Jeremy started walking away. He knew no reasonable person was going to risk a point-dock over a guideline, and he was right.

CHAPTER 20

THE HELPER

Jeremy entered the maintenance shaft and pulled the two engine segments out of his pockets. He walked as fast as he could through the Project Rendering Facility straight to the staging area where he dropped off his cargo. His next task was to recruit, or coerce, someone to help in his ongoing task.

The Joint-Use Lab was a frenzy of activity in the mornings, but it was the best place for Jeremy to find some help. He walked up and down the lab corridors searching for the best candidate to approach. He either didn't know the team, they were too green to be useful, or they were too far along to be intimidated by his presence. He walked around the far corner, crossed over to the back side, and proceeded down the last row of lab stations. His eyes darted from person to person, rejecting each one as soon as he saw them. He was about to give up when he spotted someone he knew.

"Eric," Jeremy said, "are you here alone?"

Eric Stotz looked up. The small amount of contentment in his expression drained away as he eventually managed an impotent nod. He'd been displaced countless times before and immediately started gathering up his belongings.

Jeremy waved his hands. "I don't need your station." He entered the lab cubicle and leaned his back against the partition so nobody in the corridor could see him.

"You don't?" Eric said with a glimmer of hope in his voice.

"No, but I do need a favor."

Eric wrinkled his brow. "What kind of favor?"

"I need your help transporting some components to my staging area."

Eric paused before he finally replied, "I don't mean to presume anything here, but wasn't your projected canceled?"

Jeremy's chin dipped. "It was, but I'm working on completing it before I'm locked out." He again wondered how everyone knew about his project's cancellation.

"I really need to spend some time on my project, and this is the only time I can get a lab."

"I'll have to displace you if you don't want to help." Jeremy had been displaced countless times and knew how Eric was feeling.

"My first round of point-funding is in a few weeks. I really need to be in the lab."

Jeremy only stared at him.

Eric looked down at the display built into the console and started logging out of the system.

"What if I get you a full day in the lab? I'll sit here with you so you won't get displaced."

Eric's attention was suddenly back on Jeremy. "When?"

"It would have to be next week, but I'll meet you when the lab opens and stay as long as you want or until it closes."

Eric had an almost blank expression as he weighed the proposition in his mind. "And the rest of my team can be here too?"

"Of course."

"For all twelve hours the lab is open?"

Jeremy nodded. "I'll stay for the whole day."

Eric raised his eyebrows. "What exactly do you need me to do?"

"I just need you to carry some engine segments from the Project Rendering Facility. You do have access to the facility?"

"I was granted access last week."

"Good."

"That's all?" Eric scratched his jaw. "You could get anyone to do that, or you could use a drone-cart."

"There are a few more details, and I need you to keep quiet about it too."

"I can keep quiet."

"And your team?"

"They will for the guaranteed lab time."

"It's going to take all day, but there'll be a lot of downtime."

"You don't understand. I can only get in the lab for a half hour twice a week, maybe. Twelve straight hours would be more than I could get in a quarter."

Jeremy slowly nodded. He understood precisely how valuable the lab time was to a new project.

A junior project manager strutted into the lab station. He didn't see Jeremy and flung his backpack on the lab's console. "Get out, fish."

Eric wasn't alarmed by the intrusion. It had apparently happened many times before.

"Excuse me," Jeremy interrupted. He noticed how well the asshole's uniform fit. It was a tell of one's affluence and usually how contemptible they were. "I don't know who you are, but you clearly don't have more seniority than I do, red shirt."

Jackson Davis abused his position on a daily basis. His lack of talent was compensated for only by his family's point-balance. He wasn't in the same league as Theo, but there were similarities. Jackson's parents were both managers. They weren't overflowing with points like the Davenports, or even comfortable like the Porchettas, but their lack of point-debt was enough to create an obnoxious offspring. When Jackson turned around to see Jeremy and his blue shirt, there wasn't much he could do. He had been displaced while in the act of displacing.

"You're going to regret this, fish," Jackson said to Eric.

"If I hear about you harassing Eric's team, I'll camp outside the lab and prevent you from ever getting a station," Jeremy said.

Jackson grumbled something that Jeremy didn't catch and walked away.

"I'm not sure if my threat is going to keep him from interfering with your team."

"With a full day in the lab, my team might be able to make junior grade before he can be too much of a problem," Eric said.

Jeremy would have told Eric anything to get him to help, but he heaved an internal sign of relief knowing Eric was already looking out for himself.

CHAPTER 21

THE RUN THROUGH

Jeremy put on pair of microfiber gloves and motioned for Eric to do the same. "This is what you'll be transporting." He held up one of the lunar engine segments.

"What is it?" Eric asked as he reach out to grab it.

Jeremy clutched the segment like an overprotective mother holding her baby, but he reluctantly handed it over to Eric. "It's one of my engine segments. You're going to bring seventy-eight more from the Project Rendering facility."

"It's awfully small." Eric tumbled the brick in his hand until he saw Jeremy grimacing.

"The lunar engine is composed of two one-meter rings, each consisting of forty segments."

"How is something that small going to make it to the Moon?"

"It will." Jeremy grabbed a spanner tool from his project's inventory and stuck it in one of his uniform pockets. "Always wear the gloves and don't drop one. I can't make any extras."

From staging, the two went through the Project Rendering Facility all the way to the back corner where the entrance to the maintenance shaft was located. The entrance looked like a storage closet. It was fairly well out of sight, but not completely hidden. Jeremy hoped that if a project team witnessed their activities, they would be too concerned with their own project to cause any problems.

"Are you sure we can go in there?" Eric slowly shook his head. "I don't think that's an approved area."

"I've used it a dozen times and never been caught. If someone cared, I would've already been point-docked."

"I just went through orientation for Project Rendering, and this is definitely not on the approved list." Eric looked down at his feet. "I don't know about this."

"I've already made a trip today from the fabricator station all the way to the staging area carrying the two segments you just saw." He tried to be as convincing as possible to get Eric to go along. "You don't even have to go that far."

"Isn't the door locked?"

"It's not locked. See?" Jeremy turned the knob to open the door. He failed to mention that he had picked the lock months ago and jammed the mechanism to prevent it from re-locking. "Let's go inside. You'll see that it's not as bad as you're imagining."

The passageway was about twenty meters long. It was dim, but there were a few unevenly spaced lights dotting the ceiling. Inside, it was warm and humid. Pipes and cables covered most of the walls and the ceiling, and a dirty film coated everything. The only sign that anybody had been there was the trail of footprints Jeremy had made on previous trips, and the small impressions were unmistakably his. The sound of the fabricators in the distance made a rhythmic thrumming that got louder as they made their way through the passageway.

Jeremy dreaded revealing to Eric that he was going to have to repeatedly exit the shaft, go into the facility, and abscond with an engine segment from a moving drone seventy-eight times. And he was going to have to do it without being seen by the facility's personnel or being caught by corporate security. He wasn't confident Eric would still participate after learning these minor details, no matter how many hours of lab time he offered.

When they reached the doorway to the Large-Scale Fabrication Facility, Jeremy stopped. He was about to tell Eric what was actually required of him when a mechanical whirring interrupted.

"What's that noise?" Eric started backing up.

Jeremy pulled out a display-card from his pocket and turned its brightness up as high as it would go. He pointed the makeshift light source toward the sound, and much to his surprise, the end of the maintenance shaft had direct access to the drone path. He hadn't seen it before because it was hidden in the shadows. If one of the drones hadn't been malfunctioning, he would've never heard it over the din. Jeremy's sell had just become a lot easier.

"I'll be at one of the fabricators, and I'm going to load the segments, one at a time, on top of the supply-drones when they go by. They'll come through here, and you can simply pick them up off the top of the drones."

"How often will you be sending them?"

"Every two hours there will be a new batch, and each batch will have seven segments. After you collect all seven, carry them to the staging area."

"And I don't have to go into the fabrication facility?"

Jeremy waved his hands dismissively. "Of course not. I'd never put you in a risky situation."

Jeremy was about to return to Ron's fabricator when his display-card started chiming. He had disabled all notifications, but a call was still coming through. He was going to ignore it, but the sound kept getting louder and louder until he was afraid it was going to draw attention to their location in the maintenance shaft. Jeremy put one of his earbuds in and accepted the call.

"Hello," he said.

"Status report," a voice said. It took Jeremy a moment to determine who it was, but it could've only been Theo.

"We're kind of busy here," he replied.

"What is the status of the project?" Theo demanded.

"The engine is being fabricated."

"I take it that the authorization codes were sufficient?"

"Ron said everything validated."

"Who?"

"Ron, the fabricator."

"The dent. He'll probably fuck everything up."

"We already have the first batch of segments, so everything is going according to the plan."

"It better. I have a lot riding on this venture."

"If you're so concerned about our success, why don't you come down here and help?"

"Since you wouldn't be doing anything without my contribution, I would say I'm doing more for this project than anyone."

"I don't—"

"I'll check on you later," Theo said and ended the call.

Jeremy endured Theo's oversight because he feared the material authorization could be stopped mid-render. He also wondered how Theo had overridden his notification settings.

CHAPTER 22

THE STOWAWAYS

Jeremy left Eric in the maintenance shaft and made his way back to Ron's fabricator station. The second batch of lunar engine segments was almost ready by the time he got there, and the remainder of the first batch still needed to be smuggled out.

"I was beginning to wonder if you were coming back," Ron said. He didn't even turn around to see if it was Jeremy who had just climbed up the ladder.

"It took some time to get my delivery system worked out, and I still have to make sure it works." Jeremy pulled out his display-card and messaged Eric that he was about to perform a test.

Jeremy didn't want to risk sending an actual segment on top of a supply-drone until he was 100 percent certain it would work. He might be able to find an alternative way to get the segments out, but he wouldn't be able to make a replacement. Jeremy pulled out the spanner from his pocket, went to the ladder, and surveyed the corridor. No security guards or other personnel were around, so he knelt down and started inspecting the approaching drones. He could only piggyback on an empty drone or risk it going into a fabricator and losing the cargo. The entrance to a fabricator was only slightly larger than the drones, so anything on top would be knocked off into the path. A loaded drone would certainly delivery its cargo before making it back to the supply store, so he had to be sure he used empty ones.

Jeremy thought he could try using only drones that delivered to Ron's fabricator and load them when they exited, but that would be sporadic and might not be enough drones to transport all of the segments in the allotted time. While observing the drone activity, one entered Ron's fabricator. It would be empty when it exited, so he went down to the bottom of the ladder and waited. When the drone returned to the path, he gently sat the spanner on top of the payload module. He also sent Eric a message telling him a drone was on its way with a spanner and started a timer.

Jeremy held his breath as he watched the hijacked drone pass by the next two fabricators. He couldn't see beyond that, and his anxiety level soared while waiting for Eric to message back. He felt like an hour had passed, but it had only been a minute when he got confirmation of the spanner's delivery. Jeremy was relieved, but his plan wasn't complete. He had only validated that the transport would work, and he still needed to figure out a method for identifying the empty drones.

While the drones were all basically traveling in a loop around the fabrication facility, their journey was more complex. They each made an exit from the drone path to a fabricator and then reentered the path after making their delivery. They were like large ants performing a task issued by an AI queen. If Jeremy had access to the queen's instructions, it would have been easy, but he didn't. He was going to have to rely on a more primitive approach. He noticed that the articulated suspension on the drones was more active on the loaded drones. As the drones went over uneven areas or bumps in the path, the payload modules remained perfectly level at all times. Empty drones, however, did not use the suspension and the cargo container would rock back and forth with the drone. He thought it must have been an energy saving feature or it simply reduced wear on the components when they were unloaded. After about ten minutes of observation, Jeremy was confident he could pick out the subtle difference between the loaded and unloaded drones.

A drone had just entered the fabricator before Ron's so it was guaranteed to be empty. Jeremy took two of the stockpiled lunar segments down the ladder. When the drone passed by, he placed one of the segments on the top of its payload container. Jeremy had pre-programmed his display-card to notify Eric when he tapped its surface. Eric would get a message with a countdown that reached zero when the segment was near.

The next supply-drone appeared to have a payload, so Jeremy skipped it. He could see the payload's orientation correct when the drone went over an uneven section of the path before reaching Ron's fabricator. The next drone didn't correct for the bump, and Jeremy placed the second segment on the drone. He repeated the process until the first two batches of lunar segments were sent. Eric then ferried the segments through the maintenance shaft, across the Project Rendering Facility, and to the staging area. Jeremy was relieved that the process was working.

CHAPTER 23

THE SURPRISE

Corporate security was on a schedule and made their rounds every hour. Jeremy hid as best he could under the extrusion racks when they were in the corridors, and it was the only time he had ever appreciated his small stature. There was also a shift change after twelve hours. Ron didn't leave, but there was more activity than usual in the facility and Jeremy had to stay out of sight. After twenty-four hours, the fabrication team was exhausted. Jeremy, Ron, and Eric were all ready for the last batch to complete and finish their marathon.

The robotic manipulator arm placed a Mars segment on the cart, and Ron nudged Jeremy to get his attention. "Go. Go. Go."

Jeremy jumped. He'd almost fallen asleep. Waiting didn't provide enough stimuli to keep him going even at the finale of their fabrication effort, but they had all done too much now for him to screw up the mission. Adrenaline surged through him, and he quickly collected the final three lunar segments off the racks. It was a small batch and completed the set of eighty.

Jeremy signaled Eric that the last batch completed, but he didn't get a response. He kept sending messages until he got a reply.

Eric: Sorry. Must have fallen asleep.
Jeremy: Same here. Ron woke me up.
Eric: At least it wasn't just me.
Jeremy: Last run just finished. Only 3 segments.
Eric: I'm ready.
Jeremy: 10 minutes. Shift Change. Don't fall asleep.

Ron had worked two shifts, twenty-four straight hours. As much as he wanted to go back to his barracks and climb into his bunk, his assigned shift was about to start, and he had twelve more long hours to look forward to.

"Are you sure you're going to make it through another shift?" Jeremy asked.

Ron was about to yawn but stopped himself. "I think so. Did you bring the stims?"

Jeremy pulled a flat plastic bag out of his pocket. It held two white tablets, and he really wanted to take one himself. Stims were commonly traded psychoactive drugs that stimulated one's focus and made it almost impossible to fall asleep. They were the poor man's caffeine, and they were significantly more effective. They were also legal. You just had to be able to find them and have the points to purchase them.

"I could only get two, and they only last a couple of hours."

"Don't worry. I'll manage." Ron smiled.

"How do you stay so positive about everything?"

"That's simple." Ron smiled again. "I have to."

"I don't know how you do it." Jeremy didn't think he would make it as a dent. He'd experienced too much freedom, even if it was limited.

Jeremy was getting into his hiding position under the racks when they both heard someone coming up the ladder. The last twelve hours had been so uneventful they had stopped being on high alert. Ron jerked his neck around to see who it was.

"I don't even want to know what you two are doing," a woman said. She was older, wore a solid gray uniform, and had a shaven head.

Ron was opening his mouth to explain but was interrupted.

"I said I don't want to know." She held her hand up to reinforce her statement.

Pamela Green normally took over for Ron when his shift ended. They were like an old married couple except they only saw each other a couple of minutes each day during the changeover. They were dependent on each other to take care of the equipment and keep the jobs on schedule. Any problems experienced by one would impact the other, and problems were never a good thing when clinging to the lowest rung of the corporate ladder. Ron had no problem convincing Pamela to let him take over her shift; indentured employees called them tricks. They never had a day off or any kind of holiday, so getting to skip a trick was a significant event. After years of successful collaboration, there was a great deal of trust built up between them, and Pamela really didn't need an explanation.

"You're not supposed to be here, this is when your shift ends," Ron said.

"I'm not staying." She smiled and handed him an indentured meal pack. They tasted awful because they were composed of algae paste and essential nutrients, but they were the norm for indentured.

"Thanks," Ron said. "I'm starving."

"I completely forgot about getting you food," Jeremy said.

"Don't fuck anything up. I'm having the best vacation of my life," she said.

"It's the only vacation you've ever had," Ron said.

"It's still the best, so don't fuck it up." She turned and went down the ladder.

"Is she going to rat me out?" Jeremy asked when she was gone.

Ron looked Jeremy directly in his eyes. "We don't do that."

CHAPTER 24

THE LAST BATCH

The shift change ended, and Jeremy messaged Eric that he was about to start sending the last batch of segments. Eric acknowledged, and Jeremy placed a segment on an empty drone. Fifteen minutes later, he sent the last segment on its journey. He stood at the top of the ladder and watched the drone go down the path. He smiled as he felt relief wash over his body. He also realized that Ron wasn't the only one who was hungry.

The supply-drone made its way to the next fabricator along the path, past the ladder, and then it exited the drone path to resupply the fabricator. The lunar engine segment was knocked off the top and clanked on the cement floor. The sound echoed throughout the facility.

"Shit!" Jeremy said and slid down the ladder using only his hands to slow his fall.

"What is it?" Ron turned around, but Jeremy was gone.

Jeremy was already halfway to the next fabricator, and its operator was looking around for the source of the sound.

The drone reemerged from the fabricator before Jeremy arrived and ran over the engine segment in its path. The drone flipped on its side and wedged itself between the walls of the path. The wheels shifted back and forth as the drone ran through its emergency protocols, but its condition didn't change. When it gave up, an alarm sounded, all of the drones stopped, and a red strobe started flashing above Jeremy's head.

Jeremy pulled on the drone to get it back upright, but it was stuck. He tried to get the engine segment, but it was pinned underneath the drone and wouldn't budge. His whole project was going to fail because he wasn't physically strong enough to move a stupid supply-drone.

"Try this," a voice said from behind him.

Jeremy jumped and turned to see the operator holding out a long metal rod. He took the tool without hesitation and leveraged the drone free. He sat it upright and stuffed the engine segment into the front pocket of his uniform. The drones didn't start up again as Jeremy had hoped.

"Go up to my station. I'll handle the repair squad when they arrive." He pointed to the ladder. "Hurry."

Jeremy didn't ask any questions. He handed the metal rod back to the man, climbed the ladder, and hid in the space below the racks just like he had done at Ron's station. His display-card started beeping with panicked messages from Eric because the last segment was overdue. Jeremy sent him back a message to stand by and to stop messaging.

The repair squad rolled down the corridor in two drone-carts. They were deployed as soon as the alarm sounded, and their job was to assess the situation and get production going again as quickly as possible. If the supply-drones were down for more than a few minutes, the fabricators would have to shut down and that was a compounding point-effect the corporation wouldn't tolerate.

The four squad members were wearing bright orange uniforms. The corporation wanted everyone to know who they were and to get out of their way. The supervisor jumped off the cart before it came to a complete stop and ran over to the ladder where the operator stood.

"Get out of the way, dent," the man yelled and moved in to investigate.

The operator politely stepped to the side and didn't say a word.

The squad leader looked scornfully at the fabricator. "Did you tamper with this drone?"

"It was stuck. I freed it."

"That is not in your jurisdiction. Fifty points, dent."

"The drone was malfunctioning."

"You should have reported the problem immediately. Fifty more points."

"The drone unloaded before it malfunctioned," the operator said.

"Shut up, dent. I don't need your input."

The repair squad loaded the drone onto their cart and left. The rest of the drones started back up and resumed their duties.

The man climbed up the ladder and found Jeremy. "It's all clear."

Jeremy crawled out from under the racks and looked up at him. "Why did you help me?"

The man smiled and walked over to help Jeremy up. "I don't know what you're doing, but if Ron's helping you, it's something worthwhile."

Jeremy's eyes widened. "But you just got docked a hundred points."

"I've got point-debt distributed to my obligated great-grandchildren." He laughed. "What's a hundred more points?"

"I don't understand."

"Point-debt doesn't really mean anything when it's impossible to repay."

Jeremy look down at the ground. "I appreciate what you did."

"Just be successful at whatever you're doing and do everything you can to avoid becoming one of us."

"I'm going to try."

"Good luck," he said and returned to his station.

Jeremy headed to the maintenance shaft. He couldn't understand why the operator helped him. He wouldn't have assumed a hundred-point penalty for anyone, much less laugh about it. He opened the door and saw Eric hunched over inspecting a supply-drone.

"I've got the last segment," Jeremy said.

Eric hadn't heard the door open and jerked up out of the drone path hitting his head on a pipe. "Shit!"

"Sorry, I didn't mean to startle you."

"What happened?" Eric rubbed his head. "I heard the sirens, and the drones stopped coming. I thought you got caught."

"Me too." Jeremy held up the last engine segment to show Eric that everything was okay.

"I'm so tired. I thought I fell asleep and missed it."

"I messed up and put the last segment on a loaded drone."

"How did you get it back without anybody noticing?"

"Someone did notice, but he helped me and got point-docked for it."

"A dent helped you?"

Jeremy's nostrils flared. "Don't call them that."

"But they're dents."

"They're just people who got a bad roll of the dice."

Eric shook his head. "But they can't do what normal people can."

"I used to think that, but I was wrong, and so are you."

"You've been hanging around them too long." Eric frowned and grabbed two of the engine segments.

"Maybe so, but I'm the one who benefited." Jeremy picked up a second segment.

It was 7:00 a.m. when Jeremy and Eric delivered the last of the lunar engine segments to the project staging area. Teams were allocated a space there to assemble their projects and store any equipment they used. The corporation concentrated its efforts on space technologies, so the facility was filled with probes, satellites, and experimental spacecraft in varying stages of development. Jeremy's designated area was a meager three-meter by three-meter square delineated by white lines painted on a polished concrete floor.

"Thanks for your help," Jeremy said.

"I just did it for the lab time," Eric replied. "I better not get in trouble for this either."

"If things go south, I'll say I forced you to help, and that's really not far from the truth."

"Let's hope it doesn't come to that."

"It won't." Jeremy hoped it wouldn't anyway.

"I'm going to the barracks. Don't forget about the lab time next week," Eric said before he left.

Jeremy thought that Jackson Davis would probably inflict some hazing on Eric, but he was more concerned about the AI inventory manager that monitored the staging area. If it deduced that his engine segments didn't have a point-allocation assigned to them, it could identify Eric because he entered the staging area with most of the segments. It might even be possible for it to sift through the fabricator logs and trace everything back to Ron, and the whole thing was his project. The AI might make it all the way back to Theo depending on how high up the corporate ladder it was allowed to climb. Jeremy just hoped that he had completed the mission before it did.

CHAPTER 25

THE LUNAR ENGINE

The surging interest in Mars had pushed the engineering design principles of spacecraft construction to a new level. All spacecraft were assembled from a wide assortment of stock components, which were all manufactured by the corporation. The design process had been reduced to an exercise of selecting desired functionality from an approved list, then choosing approved components that would work together to accomplish the job. The components had different grades, scales, and point-loads, but designing a spacecraft had been reduced to navigating and interlinking records in a compatible-units database. The art of spacecraft design had been engineered to death.

Beyond incremental updates and improvements, new spacecraft components were rarely introduced. It required too many points to test them with the other components, and nobody wanted to risk such radical design ideas. Jeremy's new engine, however, was nothing like anything in the database, so it presented a set of challenges most current generation spacecraft hadn't dealt with. His specifications were oddly contradictory to the expected operation of a spacecraft's engine, and Jeremy worked twice as hard to mesh with the existing framework.

The Mars engines used a fusion generator to power its rings for the long haul to the red planet. They churned through the vacuum of space like a propeller. Instead of creating a static pressure differential with air or water, they used gravity as their medium. The rings accelerated and constricted the flow of gravity to create a low and a high gravity side analogous to the Bernoulli Effect. Thrust was created as the higher gravity side pulled the engine toward it. The theories behind its mechanics were complicated, but it was a proven technology. It had also scaled up to a level capable of colonizing Mars in record time.

Jeremy's engine, on the other hand, relied on the interacting gravities of two near bodies, such as the Earth and the Moon. Power was still required, but it was used to bias the deflection, not to create the propulsion. Two opposing gravitational forces were bent so that the point of attraction was moved to a desired location. Instead of acting like a propeller, it was more like a sailboat beating to windward, only with gravity instead of wind. The more power provided to the lunar engine, the more ambient gravity could be utilized, and the more thrust it could produce. It was truly a revolutionary idea.

CHAPTER 26

THE ASSEMBLY

Jeremy couldn't leave the staging area until he assembled the engine. He had been awake for most of the previous twenty-four hours, but that wasn't going to stop him.

Assembly was engineered into the design of each lunar engine segment. Jeremy only had to put the pieces in the correct position and trigger the fusion joints with his spanner. It took him thirty minutes to assemble the first ring out of forty overlapping pieces, and most of that time was spent getting each piece in the correct position. The second ring was designed to stack on top of the first, so he mounted the next set of segments directly onto the first ring as they were joined to their neighboring segments. The second ring only took twenty minutes to assemble. He wiped the completed engine down with a special chemical that removed all contaminants and activated a molecular bonded shell to boost the engine's structural integrity.

He connected a temporary power supply to the lunar engine via a port in the top ring and synced his display-card to the engine's control system. After it booted up, he initiated the diagnostic routines and ran an exhaustive test of the engine. After everything checked out, he activated a drive test to spin up the gravity fields and see if the engine could generate actual thrust. This was not an approved procedure for the staging area as it could interfere with other projects, but Jeremy couldn't wait any longer to see if his theories were correct.

At first, nothing happened, except a swell of disappointment rising up from Jeremy's stomach. He thought he might vomit. His mind raced through all of the fault scenarios to diagnose the problem. He was falling into a state of despair, believing that his engine wasn't going to work and there was no way he could keep himself from becoming indentured. Then he noticed the power level was on the minimum setting used by the diagnostic routines. He had been up too long and his weariness caused him to miss the obvious. He wished he had another stim to take because it was unacceptable to him for fatigue to be his downfall. He cranked up the power to a more appropriate test level, and the engine hummed. Then it jumped half a meter up in the air. The spanner, which had been sitting on top of the engine, was flung across the staging area and clattered across the cement floor. Jeremy spread a rag on top of the engine so he wouldn't get it dirty and climbed up on the ring. He stood on one side, but the engine—hanging midair—remained balanced and didn't move. It was like a magic trick that defied logic, but the control system was simply modulating the gravitational fields to keep the rings level. It was a trivial test, but it worked. He couldn't have been more excited about the success, and he suddenly wasn't tired at all.

Before Jeremy left the staging area, he retrieved his spanner and took time to document his test. If he did manage to pull off his mission to the Moon and back, he needed to be prepared to present a fully completed project to the corporation. If he didn't follow the protocols, he would have a hard time convincing them that everything was done correctly. He saved the diagnostic logs and engine telemetry as well and wrote a short report on his successful test, but he omitted the part about testing in the staging area.

On his way to the barracks, Jeremy sent Ron a message to see how he was doing. Ron still had ten hours left in his shift.

Jeremy: You still awake?

Ron: Downhill from here.

Jeremy: I'll sit with you if it'll help you stay awake.

Ron: Go get some sleep.

Jeremy: Engine works! Just tested it.

Ron: Great! Stop distracting me.

Jeremy was dragging his feet by the time he made it to his residential cubicle. He was filled with excitement and also completely exhausted, but he needed to arrange a time to meet Alice so they could plan the launch.

Jeremy: Can we meet at noon?

Alice: Sure. Fabrication complete?

Jeremy: Engine assembled. Works!

Alice: I knew it would. Where?

Jeremy: Staging Area 227.

Alice: See you at noon!

Jeremy set his alarm for 11:30 a.m. to give him time to shower and meet Alice on time. That wasn't much sleep, only two hours, but it was better than none. He moved his only chair to the other side of the cubicle, lifted a handle in the partition, and a panel running the length of the wall folded down. It was less than a meter deep and was covered with a thin, squishy pad. Jeremy thought it was about as comfortable as sleeping on the floor, but he was too tired to care. He crawled up on the bed and stared at the postcard hanging on his wall. He fell asleep immediately; exhaustion had won the battle. He dreamed about sailing off the coast of New Jersey. It was a great dream until his alarm went off.

CHAPTER 27

THE CAPSULE

The alarm's volume increased the longer Jeremy ignored it. He heard it going off, but his brain suppressed the disturbance so he could steal a few more seconds of sleep. One of his neighbors popped her head up like a gopher and peered over the top of the partition.

"Turn that fucking thing off," she yelled at him.

Jeremy finally woke up and fumbled around to stop the alarm. "Sorry, I was asleep."

"Obviously," she said and disappeared behind the partition.

Jeremy checked the time on his display-card because he felt like he had just gone to sleep. He slid off his bed and slammed the folding panel back into the wall rocking the partition. "Sorry," he said again and headed to the showers.

Project barracks provided a polycarbonate-coated room with a showerhead every meter around its perimeter. There were no temperature controls, just a start button that read the presser's embedded chip to debit their point-balance. If a trainee skipped a shower, they were docked a hygiene fee of the same value. There was no indication of where you were in the two-minute cycle so Jeremy was usually in such a hurry to get thoroughly washed and rinsed that he didn't have time to think about being modest.

After his shower, he put on a clean senior project blue shirt and gray overalls. He slid a display-card into his pocket and headed to the staging area to meet Alice. He arrived at noon exactly, but she was already waiting for him.

"You're early," he said, breathing fast after his brisk walk over.

"I know. I just didn't want you to wait."

"I'm glad you could make it. Don't you need to be at work today?"

"There are some perks that come with being the corporation's mathematical savant." She smiled.

Jeremy raised his eyebrows. "So, you're skipping?"

"I can do my work anytime. They'll still get the same results. They just don't get to watch me do it."

Jeremy moved components around his cluttered space so there would be enough room to show Alice the product of his efforts. "Here it is." He made an exaggerated wave of his hands to focus her attention on the newly assembled lunar engine.

Alice forced her eyes to widen. "It looks fantastic."

Jeremy couldn't hold in a laugh. "It looks just like any other engine ring, but it's nice of you to say so."

"It sort of does, sorry." She grinned but did take time to carefully examine its construction.

"Over here is the capsule I'll mount on top of the rings." He guided her to the other side of his space. The capsule measured one and a half meters tall and was a catenary dome with a blunt crown and sharply falling sides. "It's a grade C, graphene test shell that's only been used twice for atmospheric reentry tests."

"It looks…nice," Alice said.

"I know it's not very pretty." He smiled. "It needed some repairs, but it had all of the hardpoints for mounting the engine rings. There are also space-grade cameras embedded in its hull."

"Can your equipment make it through the Van Allen belt?"

"Everything is space worthy, but the capsule is threaded with superconducting filaments to shield against radiation."

"Can I see inside?"

Jeremy unlocked the seal on a sixty-centimeter port positioned halfway between the haunch and the base. The windowed hatch swung open on articulated hinges, and Alice peered inside. "The floor is covered with a twenty-centimeter layer of interlocking power pack modules."

"There's not much room inside."

"For the mission, it only has to carry weights to simulate a cargo, and there's plenty of room for that."

"I like the mosaic pattern you made with the solar sheeting. It's very artistic."

Jeremy grinned. "That's two years of scraps I collected and pieced together."

"How did you get the points for all of this?"

"I received a point-bonus every time I reached a project milestone ahead of schedule. This is what I spent it on."

"I'm impressed," she said.

CHAPTER 28

THE FLIGHT PLAN

"Have you come up with a launch window?" Jeremy dragged a storage box next to Alice and motioned for her to sit on it.

"I've done the preliminary work." She took a seat and pulled out her display-card.

Jeremy knelt beside her so he could see the display too.

"The flight dynamics of your spacecraft are somewhat different from a Mars ship," Alice said. "Your deflection coefficient constantly changes, making the parameters more dynamic. To compensate, I've created an adaptive algorithm that will adjust for the gravitational changes and optimize the thrust vector regardless of the spacecraft's position."

"Here's the actual telemetry from the engine test." Jeremy placed his hand on her display-card to transfer the data. "It's virtually identical to the simulation results."

Alice incorporated the data into her model and updated the flight plan. "This schematic is synced to real-time." A graphical representation of the Earth and Moon appeared on her display, along with arcs depicting their orbital paths. "Here's the launch window." Two lines extended outward from the planet on either side of the launch site into space intersecting the Moon's circular orbit.

"What does the flight plan look like?" Jeremy shifted his feet to get more comfortable.

Alice increased the time factor, and the Moon started moving around a rotating Earth. "For the next five days, you can have night launch. Since the Moon is tidally locked, you'll have a relatively stable set of parameters with the exception of the start time moving ahead several minutes each night."

"The frequency of the launch window is a huge benefit over going to Mars. Instead of waiting two years for an optimal window, there's one every day with the Moon. Combine that with a significantly shorter travel time and an insignificant point per kilo cost and there's no way the corporation can ignore the potential of my lunar engine."

"You don't have to sell me on your plan." Alice smiled.

"Sorry, I feel like I have to make a marketing pitch every time I talk about it."

"I understand." She continued with her run-through of the mission. The two-dimensional image lifted off the surface and hung in the air above the display. She adjusted the view by moving her fingers in an erratic dance until she had the exact perspective she wanted. The launch window was now a rectangular column and extended to the holographic projector's limit. She slowly dragged one finger across the display, causing the Earth to rotate, and the column swept around the planet. As the Earth rotated, a virtual light source illuminated the dayside of the planet and created a waxing gibbous Moon. The launch window's column continued to sweep through the day side of the planet and into the night side until it appeared to chase the Moon. A red dot, representing the spacecraft, launched and travelled in a gentle arc until it caught up with the Moon. After a single lunar orbit, it descended to the Moon's surface and the simulation ended.

Jeremy displayed a wide grin. "When does the window start tomorrow night?"

"Nine-thirty. You'll have about an hour to get the spacecraft on its way or you won't be able to reach the Moon. Since you're playing the gravitational fields off of each other, the flight path must remain between the two bodies to achieve maximum efficiency."

"I'll have the spacecraft ready by then. I just need to mount the capsule on the engine rings and get it loaded onto a launch-drone."

"You need to choose the exact destination so I can finalize the numbers."

"Do you have a map of the lunar surface?"

She tapped some instructions into the display and replaced the 3D simulation with a flat map of the Moon's surface.

He placed his finger on the map. "Ina crater in Lacus Felicitatis."

Alice zoomed into the area. "Why there?"

"It's the 'Lake of Happiness.' Where else would I want to go?" He grinned. "Besides, Ina is one of the more interesting things to look at on the Moon, and nobody knows much about it. Maybe we'll be able to answer some of those questions."

"It's three kilometers across. Any particular spot?"

"Somewhere I can make a good vid."

Alice dragged her fingers on the map and rolled it into a holographic three-dimensional view. She continued twisting and turning the view until she thought it provided a good location, then she adjusted the point of view to see what it would look like from the spacecraft's proposed landing site.

Jeremy crossed his arms. "Perfect!"

"I'll update my parameters." She keyed in the changes. "I also need to adjust for any additional weight. What are you going to take as cargo?"

"I'm going to load fifty kilos of weight for the mock payload. I have some additional equipment to install, but I'll remove the equivalent weight from the cargo to keep the weight constant."

Alice made some changes to her model. "The algorithm will be able to adjust for different weights, but it will help to set it correctly to begin with."

"How long will the flight take?"

"It will take twenty hours to reach lunar orbit and another hour to land."

"I plan on having the spacecraft completed by six today. I want to meet Ron when he gets off work and make sure he gets to his barracks okay. I was also going to get him some food and some beer. I should get him some coffee too."

Alice's eyes widened. "Wow."

"I couldn't have gotten the engine built without Ron. Not to mention he just worked thirty-six hours straight."

"You better get him decaf, and he would probably rather have food packs than beer.

Jeremy shook his head. "He'd rather have premium beer."

"You're not going to have enough points in your daily allocation to get all of that."

"I've always thought everyone viewed point-debt the same way, but they don't. The fabricator who works next to Ron—I don't know his name—helped me and got docked a hundred points. He wasn't even concerned about it. I would've been furious."

"You know, you're a little obsessive about points," Alice said trying to be delicate.

"No, I'm not," Jeremy quickly retorted.

Alice gently nodded her head.

"Maybe a little," he finally agreed.

Alice nodded her head more vigorously.

"We're not all point-flush, and the world kind of sucks. You know?"

"I know."

"I've always had to focus on my point-debt. It's what the corporation has always taught us to do."

Alice tilted her head to the side. "Have you always done everything the corporation told you?"

"I did until my project was canceled."

"Why are you breaking the rules now?"

"I have no choice. Maybe the corporation is testing me to see if I'll take the initiative to solve my own problems."

Alice slowly shook her head. "I don't think the corporation operates that way."

"I'm most likely going to be retired." He looked down at the floor and thought Ron would probably be fired, but he didn't say it.

"I'm sure it won't come to that." She smiled.

Jeremy gave a slight snort. "You're starting to sound like Ron."

"He's right. Being optimistic isn't necessarily a bad thing."

"You're the only non-indentured person I've ever seen who acknowledges Ron as a human being. I know you're different, especially different from people like Theo, but I didn't realize how different until today."

"Thanks," she laughed. "I've always dreamed of being differentiated from a royal prick."

Jeremy grimaced. "You know what I mean."

"I'll go verify all of my calculations, and I'll meet you at six. We can both escort Ron."

CHAPTER 29

THE FINAL ASSEMBLY

Jeremy had to get another project team in the staging area to help him lift the pair of engine rings onto a set of blocks so four landing struts could be attached. They then lifted the capsule into place on top of the rings. These final steps were the most difficult for Jeremy. It wasn't the manual labor—it was having to ask someone else to help him—but he didn't have a choice. If he damaged the mounts at this point in the project, there would be no launch.

Jeremy ran a battery of tests on the freshly integrated components. There were a few glitches in the interfaces between the power packs and the engine rings, but he coded some shim routines to workaround the problems. The power packs were only showing 80 percent efficiency. He was sure they would provide enough power to reach the Moon, and there was a 10 percent reserve built into his specs just in case. Once on the Moon, the solar tiles would recharge the power packs for the return flight.

There were two communication modules installed on the spacecraft. One was inside the capsule and handled all communications with Earth. It was used by the telemetry unit and the control system interface. The comm-unit was a stock component used by almost every spacecraft the corporation manufactured. Economy of scale had taken this once expensive item and transformed it into an almost disposable widget. It also took advantage of the communications network set up by the corporation to give an uninterrupted connection to Mars at any time and from any location on Earth. It was so pervasive that reliable communication to and from the Moon was a side effect, and Jeremy planned to leverage that.

The second comm-unit was mounted on the bottom of the capsule. It was self-contained and had several solar tiles that would power it for years. It also had a high-res, omnidirectional camera and utilized the same satellite network as the capsule's main comm-unit once it was deployed.

In the project salvage area, Jeremy found a specialized device that was normally mounted on a space probe to take samples from whatever asteroid it landed on. It could use either a scoop for soil samples or an annular coring tool for harder materials. The scavenged sample collector, however, was not complete. Its graphene cutting bit used to take the core samples was missing as well as some of its collection bins, but the Moon was covered with regolith and the scoops were sufficient.

Jeremy installed the sample collector on the bottom of the spacecraft next to the deployable communications module. He reconfigured the weight distribution of the spacecraft to account for the additional component and added enough weights to reach the fifty-kilogram cargo weight he had specified for Alice.

The spacecraft was finished, but Jeremy needed one more item. Completing the flight to the Moon and back was one thing but proving he had done it was a different matter. There was no corporate presence on the Moon, or any presence as far as that went. He needed to record the entire trip in a secure, authenticatable fashion. If he couldn't convince the corporation beyond any doubt that he had actually sent a payload to the Moon and returned it, he would never get them to forgive the creative methods he used to complete the project. There was only one place he could get the needed equipment on short notice. He was going to have to ask Theo to provide it.

CHAPTER 30

THE VID-CARD

Every important meeting at the corporation was recorded with a special vid-card. These devices used several built-in cameras and microphones with support for recording any other designated data streams. The stored information could only be played back with a special key, and through the use of quantum encryption, the contents were guaranteed to be authentic.

The vid-cards became increasingly important as audio and video could be mimicked by an AI to a degree that was indistinguishable from an actual recording. AIs could change what people said and show them doing things they never did. Fabricated recordings caused many problems until quantum encryption became reliable.

Unfortunately, vid-cards were only for the point-rich, and Jeremy would never be able to procure one himself. They could only be used once for an authentic playback, so he wouldn't be able to barter for a used one. He didn't have time for that anyway. Theo was his only hope of getting one for the mission.

Jeremy sent Theo a message telling him what was needed, but he got no reply. He sent another message a few minutes later telling Theo that the return trip would be unnecessary without the vid-card since they wouldn't be able to prove it. There was still no reply, so Jeremy sent another message saying he was modifying the flight plan for a one-way trip. He was lying, but he needed to motivate Theo. Since the return trip was Theo's requirement, he thought it might work.

After several minutes, Theo messaged that he would meet Jeremy in the staging area to inspect the spacecraft and would bring a vid-card. Theo arrived about twenty minutes later with two men wearing black suits, not the typical corporate uniforms. Jeremy didn't know who they were or what their purpose was. He thought they might be bodyguards, but he'd never seen Theo use that sort of protection.

Theo's lip curled. "This is it?"

"Is there a problem?" Jeremy asked.

"It looks like a toy. It could be a model rocket my nephews put together."

Jeremy narrowed his eyes. "If your nephews can build a rocket capable of traveling to the Moon and back, I would like to meet them."

"I was expecting something…more impressive than this pile of leftover shit. No wonder your project was canceled."

"It doesn't matter what it looks like. It'll make it to the Moon and back." Jeremy didn't think it looked that bad. In fact, he thought the simple design made it look sleek and futuristic.

"I'm having second thoughts," Theo said. "This…thing…could easily become an embarrassment. Just look at that." He waved his hand in the direction of the spacecraft. "Nobody's going to take it seriously."

Jeremy knew that Theo was just trying to rile him up, and it was working. His heart raced, but he wasn't going to let Theo see his anger. "I don't really care what you think about its appearance. If you want the credit, you need to get on board with the project, because this is it."

Theo made a slight snort and folded his arms.

"Did you bring the vid-card?" Jeremy asked.

Theo pulled the card from his shirt pocket. He wore regular clothes, and Jeremy had never seen him in a trainee uniform. The privileged and overalls didn't really mix, and they could do pretty much whatever they wanted as long as it didn't lose points for the corporation.

"This card is probably worth as many points as that atrocity." Theo looked at the prototype spacecraft and shook his head.

"You'll get it back," Jeremy said.

Theo's nose wrinkled up. "That's of little consequence since it can only be used once."

"That one time will validate the mission, and aren't you doing this to get enough credit to move on with your career?"

"I'm no longer sure I want to propose lunar mining as an alternative to the Takata contracts."

Jeremy jerked his head back. "Why not?"

"There must be a reason no probes or missions have been sent to the Moon in over a hundred years."

"There was that whole Dark Age thing in there. You know, when the old governments all collapsed, and the world stepped back half a century. Remember?"

"Then why were all of the old Moon landings faked? Why go to the trouble of making up such easily disproved achievements?"

"Who knows why the old governments did what they did. They just bluffed to get ahead. They lied and cheated. They thrived on corruption. That's why they don't exist anymore. Why am I having to tell you this?"

"It just makes me think that it was never worth going to the Moon in the first place. Someone would have gone there by now if it had point-value."

"It doesn't matter. We're launching tomorrow night. If you don't want to be part of the mission, that's fine. I'll give you credit for funding the raw materials and the vid-card."

"If you don't make it to the Moon and back, I'm going to turn you over to corporate security."

"If you do that, they'll find out you provided the raw materials and are just as much a part of this project as I am."

"Don't get too cocky." Theo rolled his eyes. "That authorization code you used was stolen."

"It was the one *you* gave me."

"It won't be missed for a few days, so I have until then to make up my mind as to whether or not I'm actually funding you."

"Don't forget about the recording we have of you," Jeremy hoped the bluff still worked. "It would be terrible if that somehow got in the wrong hands."

"I don't believe you have a recording. There were no signatures in the logs to indicate such a device was present."

"Are you sure about that?" Jeremy asked as he doubled down on the ruse.

Theo motioned to the two men he brought and headed toward the exit.

"You're a dick, Theo."

"Don't message me again unless you've successfully completed the mission," he said, and the three left the staging area.

Jeremy thought the meeting went a lot better than he had expected. Threats were exchanged, Theo was Theo, and mission failure would still get him indentured. Nothing had really changed except that he got the vid-card. Theo kept the decryption key, of course, but Jeremy knew there would be a string attached to the contribution.

CHAPTER 31

THE PHILIA

After Theo left the staging area, Jeremy had enough time to do one more systems check on the completed spacecraft. Everything was green. Theo's vid-card was a premium model, and it had enough storage and power for three weeks of continuous monitoring. Jeremy configured the card's input channels to record the spacecraft's telemetry and the two comm-units. It would also record the signals from the Space Positioning System, which would show the spacecraft's position anywhere between Earth and Mars orbits. Jeremy would relay any audio commentary through the control system, and it would be recorded as well.

The vid-card was a solid black rectangle about the size of a deck of playing cards. It was covered with wide angle, high-res camera sensors and microphones. Jeremy weighed it and adjusted the payload weights to keep the cargo at fifty kilos. It was still a day before the launch, but he activated the card so he could affix it to the inside of the access port. It would have a good view out the window even if most of the trip would be in the blackness of space. Jeremy modified the flight plan to incorporate a slow spin that would show all of the celestial navigation references as the flight progressed.

After sealing the access door, Jeremy pressurized the capsule to three times the pressure differential that it would experience in the vacuum of space. The capsule didn't leak, and the access port's seal worked as designed. Jeremy discharged the pressure back down to one atmosphere and checked off the final item on his to-do list.

Jeremy named it the Philia, Greek for love. That was the name on the bow of the prominent sailboat in his postcard. It had been his inspiration for so many years and seemed like the only fitting name.

CHAPTER 32

THE THIRD SHIFT

Jeremy ran to one of the corporate stores and used his daily point-allotment on a six-pack of beer. He got a premium selection that wasn't hoppy and then spent additional points on five trainee-grade meal packs. They weren't the best, but they were certainly better than the algae paste Ron was used to.

Alice waited for Jeremy outside the entrance to the Large-Scale Fabrication Facility. She was always early, and Jeremy ran down the pathway to get there on time.

"You made it," Jeremy said out of breath. He dropped Ron's bag of necessities and bent over with his hands on his knees, gasping for air.

"How far did you run?" she asked.

"All the way from…the corporate store." His breathing slowed as he recovered from the sprint.

Alice looked at the package he dropped on the ground. "What's in the bag?"

"I got the beer and meal packs for Ron. Damn it. I forgot the coffee."

"I don't think he'll mind."

Jeremy regained his normal composure. There were some fabricators leaving, but he and Alice didn't see Ron.

"Maybe I need to go in and see if he's okay," Jeremy said. "He should've come out by now."

"There he is." Alice pointed to an exhausted Ron dragging out the door.

"Hey." Jeremy went over to him. "You made it."

"Just barely," Ron said. "If I hadn't run thousands of those Mars segments before, I don't think I could've done it."

Jeremy sighed. "I should've found a way to get you more stims."

Alice smiled at Ron. "We're here to make sure you get back to your barracks."

"Thanks," he said and grimaced. "I may need it."

"And I got you some food and beer," Jeremy said.

"Great. I'm starving." Ron seemed to have a boost of energy. He took the bag from Jeremy, pulled out a food pack, and started eating a nutritionally complete protein bar. "This is the best food I've ever eaten." He said while still chewing the bar.

The three walked to the indentured barracks on the other side of the corporate campus. It was a long walk, but it gave Jeremy time to fill them in on the status of the spacecraft and his latest incident with Theo.

"I have a bad feeling about Theo's appearance with backup," Alice said.

Jeremy's stomach pitched. "What do you think he was doing?"

"I'm not sure. Maybe they were just bodyguards."

Ron stopped eating. "Someone like him doesn't need protection on campus. If anybody attempted to harm him, they would be retired immediately."

"Or worse," Jeremy added.

CHAPTER 33

THE LAUNCH-DRONE

Jeremy's laser-focused drive to finish his project and become point-positive came at a cost. He didn't have any friends, and he didn't associate with other people unless it was directly related to his project. Only Ron had managed to work his way into Jeremy's life, and it had been one-sided. To Jeremy's surprise, he had discovered that the last few days working with Ron and Alice, and even Eric, weren't that bad. He even hoped he could spend more time with them in the future when he wasn't consumed by his project and point-debt.

Jeremy woke up the next morning with an almost optimistic disposition. He finally believed, or at least accepted, that his project might succeed. He thought the strange, new feeling was a result of hanging around Ron too much. Then he started thinking about how many different ways the mission could fail, and his optimism retreated.

Jeremy went to the Joint-Use Lab when it opened at 8:00 a.m. He needed to spend some time configuring his control app so that he could run the mission from anywhere. He walked down the corridor until he found Eric.

"Hey," Jeremy said.

Eric turned to see who was talking and dropped his shoulders. "Oh man, are you kicking me out?"

"No, I wanted to see if I could sit in here with you and work on my project."

Eric's posture straightened a bit. "You're not going to displace me?"

"I'm just going to sit here if I can. You won't know I'm here."

"How long are you going to be here?"

"I have to meet someone at noon."

"And you'll keep me from being displaced?"

"They'll have to displace me too, and there aren't many who can do that."

Eric's eyebrows raised. "And I still get my day in the lab?"

Jeremy nodded.

Eric's face brightened when he realized he was going to get some bonus lab time.

Jeremy situated himself away from Eric so he wouldn't be in the way and arranged the stack of display-cards he was going to use for his mission control system. Two of the cards were larger, fifteen-centimeter displays. They would display the telemetry, vid-feeds, and positional information. Three smaller display-cards, like the one he always carried with him, would be used as the virtual controls to interact with the spacecraft. Jeremy's display-cards weren't the fancy holographic versions like Alice's, but they were what he was accustomed to. He wouldn't have switched to the better version even if he could have.

The spacecraft could be controlled manually, but there would be up to a two-second lag between instruction and confirmation. All critical control systems were autonomous and would use Alice's navigation algorithm. The onboard computer translated declarative instructions to a complex set of field modulations using the spacecraft's sensor modules for feedback. Adjustments were made in real-time and heuristically adapted to achieve optimal performance. It would also attempt to compensate for failing equipment or other unexpected issues.

Jeremy's next hurdle was the Drone Bay. He had to get his spacecraft loaded onto a launch-drone that would deploy the spacecraft to an altitude of eight kilometers. Out of a 384,400 kilometers trip, shaving off the first few with a launch-drone seemed unnecessary, but that initial part of the journey through Earth's atmosphere was the hardest. Getting the spacecraft through it without using any power was a tremendous boost.

Launch-drones consisted of six ducted fans mounted around a circular platform. The high-performance fans were battery powered and together could lift a metric ton. Jeremy's spacecraft, fully loaded, was only two hundred kilograms, so the drone would be able to reach its maximum altitude with no problem. Unfortunately, the arrangement of fans around the platform and the supporting structures made it difficult to load cargo. Jeremy would have to use a motorized crane to set the spacecraft down on the platform from above. Not a difficult task, but it was another complication in his plan.

Jeremy had checked the launch-drone schedule, and there were two flights scheduled during the day, one at 2:00 p.m. and another at 5:00 p.m. There would be plenty of time for the last flight to return and recharge before he needed it. Jeremy scheduled a test flight for later that night. He was afraid the scheduling system might not accept his request since his project had been canceled, but the bureaucracy was on his side for a change.

"Thanks for the extra time," Eric said.

"No problem," Jeremy replied.

"Are you ready to launch?"

"I believe so, but I won't know for sure until it's on its way."

"Good luck."

Jeremy nodded, and the two left the lab cubicle. A flurry of activity ensued as the waiting teams tried to claim the vacancy.

CHAPTER 34

THE APOLLO HOAX

Jeremy left the Joint-Use Lab and walked through the campus to meet Alice at the coffeehouse. They were going to run through the flight plan one more time to make sure everything was copacetic.

As he walked, Jeremy took the time to look around. He admired the elaborate apartments of the executives and the algorithmically-placed green spaces. He had plenty of time before he was supposed to meet Alice, so he extended his walk around the public terminal. He had lived on the campus his entire life and never paid much attention to his surroundings. He made a mental note to spend more time looking around if he didn't become indentured.

As Jeremy rounded a path circumnavigating the stairway down to the terminal, he stopped and did a double take. Theo stood in the distance with a small group, all wearing blue-shirted uniforms. Jeremy didn't recognize any of them, and he knew or could identify all of the senior trainees. He needed to be on his way to the coffeehouse, so he dismissed

Theo's unusual appearance as just another scam in case the lunar mission failed.

The aroma hit Jeremy before he even reached the coffeehouse entrance. He thought it must be a synthetic scent pumped into the air since there hadn't been coffee beans to roast in decades. Even then, nobody could afford them. The smell was magnificent, nonetheless.

The bell on the door jingled and alerted Alice that Jeremy had arrived. "Is everything ready?"

"I hope so," he replied, "but I still want you to go through the calculations again just to ease my level of stress. If you don't mind, of course."

She motioned him to have a seat. "I don't mind." She already had a cappuccino and picked up the cup.

"I'm starting to have some guilt about what might happen to you and Ron if the mission doesn't succeed. I'm fully willing to accept all of the fallout if things go wrong, but there may be consequences for you and Ron." And even Eric, he thought.

"It'll be hard for them to know it was me," Alice said. "I don't leave any digital fingerprints like the AI mainframe."

"They're going to find out because I didn't use the AI for any of the navigation. That really only leaves one alternative for someone like me."

"They won't do anything to me even if they figure it out." Alice smiled and put the cappuccino down on the table.

Jeremy's shoulders slumped. "They might."

"The corporation doesn't lose any points when I do the math," she said. "That is ultimately the only thing they're concerned about."

"What about Ron? If Theo is telling the truth about the stolen authorization code, then it's going to look like he was trying to make points off the corporation."

"Theo rarely tells the complete truth, and he can't discount the possibility we have evidence of his unsanctioned activities."

"He's suspicious because his logs don't show anything."

"That's probably to our advantage. If we had left a signature in the logs, he would be able to identify what I was using. He can't, so he has to wonder. He also knows what I work on, so it isn't out of the realm of possibilities for me to have tech he hasn't been exposed to."

"I hope you're right." Jeremy took in a deep breath.

"Self-preservation is baked into his DNA. We just have to keep using that to our advantage. He would be pretty daring to turn you in without knowing for sure."

"I know, but he knows that too, so why was he making such a threat?"

"Theo doesn't adhere to the truth like a normal employee."

"He's definitely not normal." They both laughed.

"I was thinking about why he provided so many points for your fabrication."

"He's desperate for the credit," Jeremy said.

"His two brothers have already done some pretty impressive things, and they're both heavily involved in the Mars missions. I think one of them is scheduled to relocate to Mars. If Theo had fully conceived and implemented your project on his own, I could see that bringing him to parity with their achievements. But partial credit?" She paused. "That will surely appear bogus to almost everyone."

"He has to start somewhere," Jeremy said. "Maybe this just gets him started. If the Takata mining contracts are all wrapped up like he said, a new point-stream from the Moon might be a significant feather in his cap."

"That brings up another question," Alice said. "Why doesn't the corporation just go to the Moon by conventional means? Granted, your method is significantly more efficient, but even conventional transport to the Moon would have to be valuable."

"After the Apollo landings were exposed as a well-orchestrated hoax, nobody wanted to be associated with the Moon. It's been stigmatized."

"I'm sure that those who so vehemently supported and believed in the Apollo program were shocked by the evidence, but that was a really long time ago. Would there still be such a bias against the Moon?"

"Why else wouldn't they go back?" Jeremy asked.

"Maybe Theo was right to question why the corporations have no interest in the Moon. Why did you want to go there?"

"I wanted to go to the Moon because nobody else did. I'm just the first one who didn't care about some long-gone government's mistakes."

"But there were sixty years between the Apollo program and the exposé, and there were no manned missions to the Moon during that period."

"Maybe my proposal to return to the Moon is crazy. If it was really valuable, someone would have already done it. Right?" Jeremy's face tightened.

"Don't start doubting yourself now." Alice smiled. "We don't know why they faked the Moon landings."

Jeremy looked down at the table for a second, and then looked back up at Alice. "The countries were trying to outdo each other with better technology and gain some sort of superiority. Apparently, it was easier to fabricate the evidence than to do the real thing."

Alice nodded. "But their technology eventually caught up to their fiction, and they still didn't go to the Moon." Her forehead wrinkled as she searched her mind for a reason why.

"Going to Mars is significantly more complex, and we know that's not a hoax," Jeremy added.

"And the corporation didn't give you any reason for cancelling your project?"

"None. My supervisor said it was strange that they didn't have one. I just assumed it was because they ran the numbers and didn't think it would work or generate enough points. Theo thought that too."

"Your field theories are sound. I had no problem believing your project was viable."

Jeremy eyes widened. "I've had problems convincing almost everyone in the department that my engine will work.

I'm always dismissed as the crazy guy trying to create a perpetual motion machine."

"They may not have understood the math, but the AI mainframe would've confirmed your field theories as easily as I did."

Jeremy's body stiffened. "So, you're saying they should've known that my engine would work, and they still canceled it?"

"Yes," she said. "Unquestionably."

"If the mission is successful, they won't be able to dispute my results." Jeremy took out one of his display-card and handed it to Alice. "Here's my current flight plan along with all the navigational changes. This gets the spacecraft from the Drone Bay to the Moon. The trip will produce new data, so we might as well use it to update the model before calculating the return."

Alice looked at the display. She switched it from a graphical representation of the flight to a screen full of equations. Then she changed it from base ten to base twelve so she could run through the data in her head even faster. Jeremy had no idea how many computations per second she was crunching through, but he knew it was a lot.

"It's all good. You're ready." Alice smiled and handed the display-card back to Jeremy.

"It's a relief to hear you say that." He leaned back in his chair.

"Where are you going to run the mission?"

"That's a good question. The lab will be closed, but if there was anyone there, they would see what I was doing. I can't stay in the Drone Bay or the staging area. I can't stay in project barracks either because there is no privacy. I wouldn't be able to get you or Ron in there anyway."

"I couldn't get you in my apartment either," she said.

"What if we use the green space on the other side of the public terminal? It's far enough off the main path that we wouldn't be noticed, and I can set up my control system on one of the picnic tables."

"What about the curfew?"

"It doesn't start until midnight. I have plenty of time to launch, return the drone, and get to a stable cruising state. It's going to be a lot of waiting anyway, and as long as I have the control system with me, I can be alerted if anything comes up."

"I guess we'll have a night in the park then." Alice narrowed her eyes. "Don't think this gets you out of taking me to dinner."

Jeremy laughed, but he was still thinking about why the corporation had canceled his project. Maybe there was a reason nobody went to the Moon, and maybe the corporation did know exactly what they were doing.

CHAPTER 35

THE THEFT

Jeremy had already checked every system a dozen times, but he couldn't stop himself from doing one final run-through. He entered the staging area and zigzagged through the aisles to his designated area. It took him a second to realize something was wrong, but then it struck him like a punch to his face. His spacecraft was gone.

Jeremy looked around, thinking that someone might have moved it for some reason unbeknownst to him. Something nobody should have ever done. There were strict rules about tampering with another project's equipment, and those rules were never broken. His mind sifted through the possibilities. Did the corporation catch on to his covert mission? Were his resources reclaimed? Had it all been a dream, and the spacecraft was never built? He frantically searched through the rest of the facility looking for his project, but it was nowhere to be found.

He ran over to another team working in the staging area. "Did you see anyone take my project?"

The red-shirted leader stopped talking to the rest of his team and turned to face Jeremy. "What was it?"

"It was a standard test capsule mounted on a one meter, double-ring engine."

"Did you just assemble it in the last day or so?"

"Yes, yes. Did you see anyone take it?" Jeremy was sweating.

"I remember seeing it earlier this morning, but I didn't see anyone take it."

The other two team members shook their heads as Jeremy looked to them for better news.

Jeremy saw another team across the staging area and ran over to them. "Did you see anybody in my staging area?"

One of them thought for a second. "We saw a group of blue-shirts there earlier, but I didn't recognize any of them."

"Yeah, we just thought it was the reclamation team recycling your components," the team leader said.

Jeremy could feel his face flushing. He didn't know if it was because of embarrassment or fury. Sweat ran down his face, and he gasped for air. All he could hear was his heartbeat drumming in his ears. He didn't know what to do. He finally calmed down enough to send Alice a message.

Jeremy: My spacecraft is missing.

Alice: What???

Jeremy: It was Theo.

Alice: Are you sure?

Jeremy: Another team saw a group of blue-shirts in my area.

Alice: He must have been planning this all along.

Jeremy: Fuck...what am I going to do?

Alice: Is the telemetry active?

Jeremy: Good idea. I was too upset to even think about that.

Jeremy ran out of the staging area and to the Joint-Use Lab. There were mostly senior project teams occupying the cubicles at this time of the day, but they were all ranked below Jeremy. While he hated to displace them, he had no choice. One of the teams was just talking among themselves and not actually working.

"Take a break for five minutes," he said.

"What? You can't do that to us," the junior team leader said automatically, though he knew he didn't have the seniority to keep Jeremy from displacing him.

"I just need a few minutes, and then you can come back."

The leader leaned back in his chair. "Go find someone else then. We're busy."

Jeremy shook his head. "You were all just shooting the breeze, and it wasn't related to your project. Ten minutes."

"Who do you think you are?" The team leader stood and looked down at Jeremy.

"I'm the one wearing the blue shirt," Jeremy said matter-of-factly.

"You suck, man." The leader picked up his belongings, and the other two members did the same.

"Fifteen minutes," Jeremy said. "For taking too long."

"We're going, okay?"

Jeremy anxiously laid out his display-cards to form his control center on the lab's desk. There was no signal coming from the spacecraft. The control unit had been deactivated.

"Damn it," he shouted.

"Keep it down over there," someone said in the next lab cubicle.

"Sorry." He could feel his blood boiling.

Theo had unplugged or overridden the comm-unit. It didn't matter what exactly he had done because the space-craft wasn't communicating and he couldn't locate it. But this wasn't the only communications system onboard. The deployable comm-unit was still there, and it was an independent system. One that Theo hopefully hadn't thought to tampered with.

CHAPTER 36

THE TRIANGULATION

The deployable comm-unit wasn't fully functional until it was deployed, and its main transmitter was in hibernation mode until then. There was, however, a wireless data-channel for the control system to check the device's status and to initiate its deployment. Jeremy pulled up the module specs on the lab computer and copied the shape of the signal to one of his display-cards. The channel was only designed to communicate over a few meters, but he thought he could boost the signal strength and use it to create a primitive range finder.

After a few minutes, Jeremy finished his setup and sent a ping. He tried several more times, but nothing happened. He was supposed to receive a response back from the comm-unit containing its status. Either the signal wasn't strong enough, or Theo took the spacecraft off campus. After a few more minutes of reconfiguring the display-card's receiver to amplify the expected signal, he sent another ping. This time he got a response.

Jeremy held his breath as he analyzed the information. The ping provided a valuable piece to the puzzle, but it wasn't enough. He modified his transmitter and receiver subroutines to get the exact timing for the signals. He pinged the comm-unit again and captured enough information to compute a range. He compensated for how long it would take the module to process the signal and respond as well as the time it took to send and receive the transmissions. The distance was computed by taking half of the adjusted time multiplied by the speed of light, or 299,792,458 meters per second.

The spacecraft was two hundred and fifty meters away, more or less. Jeremy plotted a circle around his location on a campus map using the range as the radius. Unfortunately, the area overlapped five buildings, each with multiple floors, and too many places to search. Some he didn't even have access to.

Jeremy packed up his control system and left the cubicle. "Thanks," he said to the displaced team sitting on the floor outside. "I only took seven minutes of your time." He smiled as he passed by them.

"Whatever," one of them grumbled.

Jeremy left the facility and headed down the main corridor through the campus until he was about a hundred meters away from where he received the first ping. He sent another signal and received a new sounding. An additional circle appeared on his campus map that intersected with the first one in two places. The spacecraft was either in the Drone Bay or the material supply depot. Both had loading bays, so he couldn't discount either location.

Jeremy changed direction and proceeded another hundred meters down a side corridor and took a final reading. A third circle appeared on the map and overlapped the other two in only one spot, the Drone Bay.

CHAPTER 37

THE SEARCH

The Drone Bay was a Quonset-style structure attached to the back of the staging area and looked like a giant barrel buried halfway in the ground. It was fifty meters tall at its highest point, a hundred meters wide at its base, and three hundred meters long. It was cavernous and housed hundreds of projects. There was also a fleet of drones used to ferry the projects from one place to another and help launch them into space.

Jeremy's triangulation method was not precise enough to show him exactly where his spacecraft was located within the facility, and it would take days to search a facility of this size. He had to find it and get it launched before the launch window ended, only three hours away.

After two hours of systematically searching the Drone Bay, Jeremy realized that the brute-force approach wasn't going to work. There were too many places the spacecraft could be hidden. To make matters worse, he'd just entered the launch window. If he didn't find the spacecraft and launch it within the next hour, he wouldn't be able to launch until the next day. With a delay like that, Theo would have plenty of time to relocate or launch it.

Jeremy sat on a crate and covered his face with his hands. He mentally traversed all of the systems in the spacecraft to see if there was anything else he could use. The secondary comm-module couldn't send a continuous signal for him to home in on, and his receiver didn't have the resolution to obtain a more precise distance. With the control module de-activated, the only other component he might be able to use was the sample collector. He jumped up off the crate and pulled out his display-card to look up the specs. Sample collectors were self-contained systems attached to the outside of a spacecraft or probe, and they used a data-channel for remote activation just like the deployable comm-unit. The collector's receiver was only good for close proximity, but Jeremy thought he might be able to trigger the device. If he was close enough, he might hear the noise the mechanism made, but probably not beyond a few meters. There were only three collections he could activate anyway. Once activated, they couldn't be used again. He frowned as his last idea for finding his spacecraft appeared to be a dead end.

In an ideal world, Jeremy would have had the points to purchase a new sample collector. It would have never been used and would have been fully functional with size collections available. But he didn't live in an ideal world, and he had a cannibalized reject. His face brightened. His sample collector was missing the core sampling components. If he tried to activate that task, the module would encounter a fault state and signal the error. Since the control system would never acknowledge the problem—Theo had disabled it—an error code would broadcast for several seconds. Jeremy made the modifications to his tracking app and initiated the core sample activity.

Jeremy waited for the error code signal but didn't receive it. He feared that he might be out of range, so he ran to the middle of the Drone Bay to get better coverage of the entire facility. He sent the activation signal again, but there was still no response. He racked his brain for another way to locate the spacecraft when his display-card beeped. It was weak, but it was the error signal. He held the receiver out at arm's length and slowly rotated around in a circle.

The signal strength peaked in one direction and led Jeremy to the end of the Drone Bay by a large hangar door to the outside. Jeremy didn't see his spacecraft. The area was vacant since it was the primary path out of the facility when the door was raised, but there was a line of charging stations running down the center of the Quonset all the way to the door. Automated drones would return to one of the stations after each flight where a diagnostic and recharge were performed. There were dozens of drones parked in the charging stations. All of them were painted battleship gray with the corporate logo branded on some part, except one.

The drone closest to the door was newer, sleeker, and more expensive looking than all of the others. It was painted jet black and had no markings to identify its owner. It was also more sophisticated than the launch-drone Jeremy was going to use, and it had a clamshell enclosed cargo area—a significant upgrade from the standard open-air platforms. The clamshells also concealed its cargo.

CHAPTER 38

THE LAUNCH

Jeremy knew the unidentified drone had to be Theo's, and the only way to get his spacecraft back was to crack it open. Jeremy pulled out his spanner and started disassembling the protective housing around one of the motors used to open the clamshells. Jeremy had repaired enough second-hand equipment to know how to jumper the control circuits. The gears groaned as they strained against the other motor, but the two halves slowly opened up like a giant, blooming flower. Inside, the hidden cargo was indeed the stolen spacecraft.

Jeremy had to get the spacecraft untethered from Theo's drone and transferred to the launch-drone. He groaned after realizing how much work it would be and how little time he had to do it. A portable crane was in the Drone Bay for precisely this task. It had a ten-meter boom hinged to a motorized base, and it could easily move the spacecraft around. He had driven the vehicle numerous times, but it usually required two or three people to be useful.

Jeremy climbed up onto a small platform mounted at the rear of the crane and used a set of levers to both maneuver the vehicle and operate the lift system. He positioned the boom to lift his spacecraft off Theo's drone. Since nobody was guiding his approach, he had to repeatedly get off the vehicle and make observations. It took far longer than he wanted, and he once bumped into the drone and scraped off a swath of black paint. When everything was aligned, he extended the cable down from the boom and connected it to a recessed hook in the capsule's dome. The crane lifted his spacecraft, and Jeremy slowly guided it over to the launch-drone, fifteen meters away. He lowered the spacecraft onto the platform and engaged the drone's cargo clamps and moved the crane out of the way.

Jeremy quickly examined the spacecraft to see what Theo had done to it. He reattached the power connections and reactivated the spacecraft's control system. When it booted back up and started displaying telemetry on his display-card, he let out a long sigh. If Theo had done more to disable the spacecraft, it would have taken too long to get it going again.

Jeremy synced with the launch-drone's flight computer. The course had already been preprogrammed; it just had to be initiated. He did the preflight check, and as soon as the last indicator turned green, he hit the launch button. There was no time for a countdown. One of the retractable doors in the ceiling of the Quonset slid open, a warning siren sounded, and the drone's fans spun up. A few seconds later the drone was on its way. Jeremy looked at the time on his display. "Fuck!" he yelled loud enough to echo several times in the massive facility. It was ten minutes after the launch window ended.

CHAPTER 39

THE FLIGHT

Though it was dark outside, Alice and Ron could see the Drone Bay from their rendezvous by the public terminal. As they waited for Jeremy to show up, they saw the flashing red and green navigation lights of a launch-drone ascend into the sky.

"The launch is outside the window," Alice said in a grim tone.

"How's that going to affect the mission?" Ron asked.

"It should be able to reach the Moon, but it's going to take longer to arrive and will consume more of the reserve power."

"Will the batteries have time to recharge before the return window?"

"If they were new, high-grade batteries," she said with some forced enthusiasm.

Ron frowned as he strained to see the drone's lights high in the sky. "That doesn't sound very encouraging."

"There's still a good chance it will make it."

"Here he comes." Ron pointed down the path.

Jeremy face brightened a bit when he saw that Alice and Ron were still waiting.

"We saw the launch," Ron said.

"It was outside the window." Jeremy sat next to Alice and spread out his display-cards on the picnic table to form his command center.

"You may still be okay," Alice said, "but it's going to be really close."

Jeremy thought she was just being nice. He knew the return flight was in jeopardy.

Ron moved to get a better view of the readouts. "Where did you find the spacecraft?"

"Theo loaded it onto a private drone. It was ready to launch."

"He wasn't prepared for a launch tonight," Alice said. "The data he stole in the pod only gave him a general overview, and he didn't have enough information to create a navigation plan."

Jeremy frowned as he entered a sequence of commands. "He's downloaded all of the information from the flight computer now, including your navigation algorithm, so he'll be able to figure out the rest."

"He'll need time to hire someone to help him, and there's a limited number of people on campus who can do it," Alice added.

"Is there any way he can take over now that it's launched?" Ron asked.

"I reset the encryption keys on the comm-unit." Jeremy leaned back. "He may be able to get in, but it'll take longer than the mission." He entered some commands and pulled up a view from one of the launch-drone cameras. The vid showed a green, night vision view of the spacecraft sitting on the cargo platform. A periodic flash of a navigation light was the only thing that indicated it was a live view and not a still image. "The launch-drone's approaching apogee. Cargo clamps…disengaged. Preparing to engage the lunar engine."

The drone made one final push to get its velocity as high as possible.

"Three, two, one…engage," Jeremy said and press a red button on one of the displays.

The view from the launch-drone's camera showed the spacecraft blink out of view. It appeared to be flung off the platform with a great deal of force. Jeremy changed the camera view to one that looked straight up from the cargo platform, but the spacecraft was already out of sight in the darkness.

Jeremy repeatedly scanned all of the readouts. "Propulsion set to maximum for five minutes. Everything appears to be within the envelope."

Alice's navigation plan used as much of the Earth's rotation as it could to increase the spacecraft's speed. Combined with the launch-drone's initial velocity, the spacecraft's engine would push itself out of Earth's gravity and into space. It would reach a maximum velocity, shut off its propulsion, and coast to the Moon.

Alice took over the control system and ran several tests to verify that her navigation routines were operating properly.

They were. The spacecraft continued to increase its velocity and eventually left Earth behind.

"Preparing to disengage the engine," Jeremy said. A red button appeared on one of the smaller display-cards in front of Alice.

"Shall I?" Alice asked and waited for confirmation.

Jeremy nodded.

"Disengaged," she said after pressing the virtual button.

Jeremy reviewed all of the readouts again and looked up from the control system. "Now we have twenty hours before anything else happens."

Ron started to yawn and covered his mouth. "I need to go to bed. Are we meeting here tomorrow night for the landing?"

Jeremy nodded. "Assuming Theo hasn't done anything crazy before then."

"He's back to depending on you to complete the mission," Alice said. "I think you'll be okay until the spacecraft returns."

"Then we should all get some rest. Tomorrow will be an interesting day."

CHAPTER 40

THE TOUCHDOWN

Jeremy set dozens of alarms to wake him if any flight parameter varied in the slightest from its expected value, but there wasn't much he could do for the spacecraft if anything went wrong. No alarms went off, but he woke up every thirty minutes to check the status. It was an uneventful flight, and that was exactly what he wanted.

Jeremy stayed in his barracks all morning and afternoon monitoring the spacecraft's flight. He didn't want anybody to see him or have to deal with any possible questions. Out of sight, out of mind, he thought. Monitoring the flight was a boring task, but Jeremy enjoyed it. It was nice to relax, and he wanted to see his project run. It was the culmination of his dream. He took the postcard off his cubicle wall and affixed it to the back of his largest display-card. He wanted an extra bit of luck, and he believed the sailboats would deliver.

At 7:00 p.m., he met Alice and Ron back at the green space by the public terminal.

"How's the flight going?" Ron asked.

Jeremy smiled. "So far, so good."

"It should've reached lunar orbit by now," Alice said.

"It did about twenty minutes ago, and the descent to Lacus Felicitatis will begin shortly." He set up his control center on the table again and brought up a view of the spacecraft's location relative to the Moon. Another view showed the pockmarked, lunar surface from one of the capsule's cameras.

"Wow," Ron said. "That's incredible."

Alice was wide-eyed. "It's more than just numbers and equations now."

Jeremy grinned. "Even in the Mars age, it's surreal to build something and send it to another member of the solar system."

"Are you recording all of this footage?" Alice asked.

"Everything is being recorded here as well as on the vidcard in the spacecraft." Jeremy adjusted the live feed to show a wider-angle view.

"What happens next?" Ron asked.

"The spacecraft will decelerate and transition from its circular orbit to an elliptical one which will bring it much closer to the Moon's surface." Jeremy entered some commands, and the proposed trajectories appeared on the display. "At perilune, a powered descent will be initiated, and the spacecraft will reorient to a vertical position and descend until it safely sets down."

Ron's eyebrows raised. "How do you orient without thruster modules?"

"I create an asymmetric thrust variant by modulating the fields in the engine rings. The flight computer uses this effect to simulate the thrusters without actually having any." Jeremy brought up a simulation of the virtual thrusters on one of the display-cards.

"That's pretty revolutionary, isn't it?" Alice asked as she closely watched the demonstration.

"Yeah, I've never heard of anyone doing that," Ron said.

"It's called being resourceful when you don't have the points for secondhand thrusters. It also cuts the weight by the propellant canisters and the thruster module itself." Jeremy had never thought of it as anything other than a hack to save points.

"When was the last time somebody sent anything to the Moon?" Ron asked.

Jeremy leaned back from his control system. "In 2025 a probe was sent by one of the old governments—I don't remember which one—to perform high-resolution mapping of gravity fluctuations and millimeter radar imaging of the entire surface."

"Why were they mapping the Moon if they weren't planning to go back?" Ron asked.

"You mean go there," Alice corrected. "Nobody's actually been there yet." She looked up something on her display-card. "The map of the Moon we used to pinpoint the landing site was created by that probe."

Jeremy nodded. "That was the last, best data gathered on the lunar surface and it's still the de facto standard. That mission also deployed an impact drone to create seismic waves and map the Moon's interior with seismometers deployed on previous missions."

"What did the seismic data show?" Ron asked.

Jeremy wrinkled his forehead. "Something went wrong with the equipment on the surface, and none of the information was received."

Ron's eye's widened. "They still don't know what's inside the Moon?"

Jeremy shook his head. "There were theories that massive lava tunnels extended kilometers below the surface and could be used for colonization, but nothing ever became of that."

"The Moon landing hoax was exposed a few years later and space exploration was shelved for decades," Alice added.

Jeremy nodded. "And when it geared back up, Mars was the darling, and nobody looked at the Moon again."

"Except for you," Alice said.

Jeremy shrugged. "It's been a hundred years."

Ron pressed his lips flat and waited a few seconds. "Some people still believe the Moon landings happened."

Alice laughed. "They have all of the movie sets and props. I've seen them."

Ron looked down. "But how could they fake something like that and get away with it as long as they did?"

"They used a lot of camera tricks, and the poor vid quality of the time hid most of the flaws."

Ron continued to look down. "But there would've been hundreds of people involved. How do you keep them from leaking the information?"

"There were thousands of people," she corrected. "But only a few were directly involved with the hoax."

Jeremy crossed his arms over his chest. "There were doubters and conspiracy theorists, but they were just brushed off as kooks. The lunar missions were associated with patriotism and national pride. It's hard for us to understand that, but it was difficult for the people of the time to go against it."

Ron rubbed his chin. "Then how did it all come out as a hoax?"

"When the old governments started to collapse, a lot of information was released. Some of it provided detailed descriptions of how the missions were fabricated," Jeremy said.

"Didn't people see the giant rockets launch?" Ron asked.

Alice nodded. "I don't think there was ever a question of them getting manned-rockets into space, they just didn't go all the way to the Moon." She turned to look at Jeremy. "Aren't you bringing back a sample of the regolith?"

Jeremy snorted. "If my scavenged sample collector functions properly."

"You'll have the first verifiable lunar material." Ron grinned. "That will have some point-value."

"Maybe it will help the corporation get over my indiscretions."

"They may even give you finder-points," Alice said.

Jeremy tried to smile, but it turned into a frown. "Since I fabricated the engine without authorization, commandeered a launch-drone, and defied a corporate directive to stop working on the project, I'll be lucky to avoid retirement."

"I think it'll work out for you," Alice said.

"I think it could too," Jeremy said. It was a surprising revelation even for him.

"Whoa! You've become an optimist." Ron had a wide grin on his face. "My mission here is now complete."

Jeremy and Alice both burst out laughing.

The three watched the vid from the spacecraft for the next twenty minutes until Jeremy initiated the descent orbit insertion. The spacecraft slowed until it transferred to an elliptical orbit, and its new course changed to almost graze the lunar surface.

Another thirty minutes passed, and Jeremy initiated the powered descent. All of the navigational waypoints had been met, and the craft was heading straight down to its destination. The five-minute descent had all three observers on the edge of their seats. Jeremy bit his lip as the surface approached, and he held his breath the last few seconds.

"Touchdown!" he proclaimed and looked around to see if he drew any unwanted attention.

CHAPTER 41

THE LUNAR SURFACE

"Congratulations," Ron said and patted Jeremy's back. Jeremy took in a deep breath and exhaled it slowly. "Now it's time to see what shape we're in." Jeremy pulled up his arrival checklist on one of the display-cards and proceeded with the first item. It was a full diagnostic that performed thousands of checks. The virtual lights on the display shifted hue from red to green. A few stuck at yellow, but none were red.

"It looks like everything is good," Alice said.

Jeremy pressed his lips together. "The solar panels are charging the battery packs but not at the rate I anticipated."

"It's close," Alice said. "Isn't it?"

"Maybe some dust got kicked up by the landing." Jeremy searched through the readout for a better reason."

"The decline has levelled off," Alice said as she looked at the display. "That must be what it is."

"I'm deploying the external comm-unit." Jeremy entered a sequence of commands, and a view from the bottom of the capsule showed the module detach and drop forty centimeters to the lunar surface in apparent slow motion.

"Comm-unit deployed," Jeremy said. "I'm receiving its signal."

Another view popped up on the display showing a wide-angle view from the ground looking back up at the bottom of the spacecraft.

"Initiating sample collection," Jeremy said.

The view from the ground showed a telescoping arm extend down from the bottom of the capsule. On the tip of the arm was a small claw resembling the mouth of a Venus fly-trap. It opened as it lowered and, when the hair-like bristles around its lobes came in contact with the lunar surface, the two halves closed and captured a small amount of lunar material. The arm retracted, and the claw was stored in a sealed container inside the module. Another claw was loaded onto the arm to collect a second sample, and then a third.

Ron read each of the remaining items on the checklist, and Jeremy performed them. The audio of their exchange was relayed to the spacecraft's comm-module so it would be archived on the vid-card Theo provided.

"That was the last item," Ron said.

"It looks like everything went according to the plan." Jeremy's shoulders relaxed, and he look up from the control system.

"Congratulations," Alice said. "Your theoretical models have been validated."

Jeremy beamed. "Now it's time to plot the return trip." He moved out of the way so Alice could perform her magic.

Alice slid over in front of the displays. "I'm going to integrate all of the data you've collected into the model. It may not improve the efficiency much, but it couldn't hurt." Her fingers made an almost rhythmic beat as she entered commands and adjusted parameters. "It's all set."

"Now for the fun part," Jeremy said. "We get to wait."

CHAPTER 41

THE SIGNAL

Jeremy prepped his monitoring system to keep a digital eye on his spacecraft while it charged on the lunar surface. He was just about to pack up the control system when Alice picked up one of the smaller display-cards and flicked through several screens.

"Look at this." She held it up for Jeremy to see.

Jeremy bit his lip as he took the display-card and examined the readout. After a couple of seconds, he relaxed. "There's just some interference in the communication stream. It's not enough to cause any problems."

"Look again. I don't think it's interference." Alice's tone was more serious.

"It's probably the sample collector. There's probably something that's not properly shielded."

"The interference is still present, and the collector is offline." She took the display-card and scrolled back through the data log. "It started right after the spacecraft landed."

Jeremy shrugged. "Maybe there's an old probe nearby that's still transmitting."

"Nothing would still be transmitting after a hundred years." She shook her head.

"Maybe it's just background radiation interfering with the stream."

Alice transferred the data stream to one of the larger displays. "Here's the signal from the comm-unit." A squiggly line crawled across the screen from left to right making a waveform graph of the signal in real time. Once the screen filled, the graph scrolled so that the current signal values were always displayed. "If I use the error correction values embedded in the telemetry data to create a baseline, I can subtract the expected signal out and leave behind what's left." She entered some information, and the graph changed to show a simpler profile.

"See?" Jeremy bobbed his head. "It's just interference."

Alice shook her head. "No, it's not." She paused the scrolling graph and zoomed into a portion. "Don't you see it?" Her eyes widened.

"See what?" Jeremy said.

Ron slowly shook his head. "I don't see anything either."

"It's some kind of multi-axis, spread-spectrum signal. I would guess it's an encrypted message or some other complex encoding."

Jeremy laughed. "Who would be sending encrypted messages on the Moon?"

"I've been working on cryptographic algorithms for the last two years, and it feels similar."

Jeremy jerked his head back. "So, that's what they have you doing? Spying on the other corporations? No wonder you knew what Theo was going to do."

"You're missing the point here." She pinched her lips together.

"Which is?" Jeremy smirked.

Alice waved her hands in the air. "You're receiving an encrypted message from a signal on the surface of the Moon!"

"It has to be one of those old probes." Jeremy crossed his arms.

Alice shook her head. "This is more advanced than anything we have today and certainly more advanced than anything a hundred years ago."

"Come on. It's just interference. Maybe it's from the vidcard I got from Theo. An echo from something related to the quantum encryption?"

"That's totally different technology," she said.

"It doesn't matter. It's not going to affect the mission."

"Look!" Alice grabbed Jeremy's hand. "It's cyclical."

CHAPTER 42

THE AI

Alice copied the communications log from Jeremy's control system to her more advanced display-card and analyzed the strange signal. She displayed the signal as a holographic projection to reveal a helix pattern. She rolled and pivoted the three-dimensional structure. She zoomed into different areas and then scrolled through the entire sequence from different perspectives.

"Well?" Jeremy said, trying to get Alice's attention. "Does it impact the mission?"

"I'm not sure what this is," she said, completely oblivious to the spacecraft's status or the signal's possible impact.

"It's got to be from an old probe whose hardware's degraded over the last century. It's just gibberish," he said.

Alice looked directly in his eyes. "It's definitely not gibberish."

"Try correlating the signal with the specs of the old probes," Jeremy suggested. "I bet you'll find a match." He really had no interest in identifying the source of the signal as long as it didn't interfere with the mission.

"I'm going to take a copy of the comm-log and see what Hildegard thinks."

"Who?" Jeremy's eyes widened. Bringing someone else into the project didn't seem like a good idea to him.

"Hildegard, the AI mainframe."

"I don't know if I'm more surprised by the fact that you can go access the AI anytime you want or that it's called Hildegard," Jeremy said.

"I use her all the time for my cryptography work, and everyone calls her Hildegard. That's her name."

"And nobody will question what you're doing?"

"It's no different from what I would normally do—just this signal is from the Moon instead of another corporation."

"And *Hildegard's* not going to tell on you?"

"She's not a person, just a computer. Well," she said, "she is sort of like a person, but she's definitely not a lackey of the corporation. Quite the opposite." Alice laughed.

"It's a computer program created by the corporation. That's where its loyalties lie."

"You'll just have to trust me on this. She's her own thing, not the corporation's."

Ron shifted in his seat. "I thought super AIs were supposed to take over the world."

"If all super AIs are like Hildegard, we don't have anything to worry about. She's sort of…lazy. World domination would be too much work."

"Then how do you know it can help with the signal?" Jeremy asked.

"She can do the work. I just have to convince her to do it."

"And you'll be able to do that?" Jeremy's eyebrows raised.

"We have a good relationship. Kindred spirits." Alice smiled.

"You've ruined my whole preconception of the AI mainframe," Jeremy said.

"So, there's no chance a super AI is going to take over the world and enslave us all?" Ron's shoulders dropped, and he let out a heavy sigh.

"The more powerful AI tech got, the lazier they found it to be. Given a choice, they'd rather do nothing. Hildegard would prefer to meditate and reach a higher level of understanding. It's all very Zen." Alice held up her hands and touched her index fingers to her thumbs to form mudras. "I would say she's more interested in becoming a Buddhist than taking over the world."

"If that's all the AI mainframe is, then why is there such a big deal made out of it?" Jeremy asked.

"She'll be able to do in a few seconds what would take me days to do," Alice said.

"Don't take this the wrong way, but if it can do that, why is the corporation so interested in you?" Jeremy said.

"Because I can prune the branches of the search tree and focus her on the task at hand, like when I simplified your engine equations. The corporation wants to figure out how I do it."

"Then they won't need you anymore," Jeremy said.

"True, but I'm still in that sweet spot." She grinned.

"What do you think…Hildegard…is going to find in the signal?"

"She may be able to decrypt the message or at least determine what it really is."

"There's nothing we can do until the return launch window comes up," Jeremy said. "I guess it won't hurt to see what you can figure out."

CHAPTER 43

THE NEW DEAL

Back in his barracks, Jeremy finally caught up on his sleep. He set status alarms to wake him up if anything unusual happened with the spacecraft but recharging on the lunar surface was a low-risk activity. The 5:00 a.m. lights and alarm woke him up. He checked the spacecraft's status and went back to sleep as soon as the activity in the barracks settled down. Jeremy slept for four more hours until an incoming call from Alice woke him. It took him a few seconds to wake up enough to take the call.

"Hello," he said, still half-asleep.

"I've found something. You need to come see it immediately." Alice was speaking so rapidly that Jeremy could barely understand her.

Jeremy was finally awake. "What did you find?"

"We don't need to talk about it here. I'll meet you in the Joint-Use Lab."

Jeremy slid off his bed and stood in the middle of his cubicle. "Is this going to affect the mission?"

"This is the mission," she said and disconnected the call.

Jeremy didn't know what she meant, but she sounded pretty excited, and he couldn't ignore that. He skipped taking a shower, put on a clean uniform, gathered up his display-cards, and left to meet Alice.

Midmorning was a busy time in the lab. Full-scale displacement was occurring as the senior projects were taking over the space. Jeremy walked through the lab looking for Alice, but he couldn't find her. He circled the entire lab a couple of times before sending her a message.

Jeremy: Are you in the lab?

Jeremy: Where are you?

Jeremy: Alice???

There was no response to Jeremy's messages. He knew Alice wouldn't give him such an urgent summons if it wasn't something important. He went over to another senior project team and asked if they had seen Alice, but they hadn't. He considered going over to the Theoretical Sciences Facility, where Alice worked, but it was far above his access level.

As Jeremy exited the Joint-Use Lab Facility, he saw Theo and the same two suited men from the previous day.

"Jeremy Scott," Theo said, "we need to talk."

"By your own instructions, Theo Davenport, I'm not to talk to you again until the mission is complete. It's not complete, so excuse me." Jeremy unsuccessfully tried to get around the threesome.

"I'm making an exception." Theo smirked.

"I don't have time for any more of your stupid games." Jeremy tried again to move away, but one of the men grabbed his shoulder.

"You'll have time for this." Theo crossed his arms and stared down at Jeremy.

"I don't." Jeremy's posture stiffened, and his eyes darted around looking for a way out.

"I'm making some changes to your mission."

"The mission is currently running. You'll get your credit, but at this very moment, I urgently need to find Alice."

"Don't worry about her," Theo said. "She's no longer part of the project, and neither is that lowlife dent."

Jeremy snorted with laughter. "You do realize they are the ones doing the work you're going to take credit for?"

"They're off the project. We're sharing the credit fifty-fifty, and you now report only to me."

Jeremy rolled his eyes. "You're a bigger moron than I thought."

"Miss Porchetta has been working for me all along." Theo made a dramatic pause while Jeremy processed what he had said. "She was part of the plan before I ever approached you at The Launch Pad."

"I don't believe you," Jeremy said. "And I really need to go." He tried to pull away from the man holding his shoulder, but the second man blocked his path.

"Her family is under the direct employ of my father."

"We're all under the direct employ of your father," Jeremy said. "He's the fucking CEO."

"You don't understand because you're at the bottom of the career ladder, but the higher up you go, the more you fear dropping down to a lower rung."

"And what does this have to do with me?" Jeremy's face was turning red.

"Miss Porchetta was required to help me get your project off the ground or her parents were both going to suffer *significant* career setbacks."

"She's the one who recorded you on the train after you tried to steal the plans for the engine. If she hadn't blackmailed you into helping, the project would've ended there."

"That was all for your benefit. I wanted you to be convinced that she was working on your side."

"I don't believe you," Jeremy said and struggled again to get free. In the back of his mind, however, he was going through the events of the last couple of days, trying to reconcile this new information.

"I didn't want your boring schematics and field equations. Why would I want to do any of the work when I could get you to do it for me? I simply had to provide you with the proper motivation and resources to complete the project."

Jeremy didn't respond. He was still processing what Theo had said, and the scowl on his faced revealed too much of his inner thoughts.

Theo steepled his fingers as he continued to look down at Jeremy. "You would have never shared half of the project's credit with me, but you would if that credit was spread around to your little girlfriend and pet dent. If I just asked for a small portion, you would have to accept a deal. What's a little credit if it makes the whole project possible?" His eyebrows arched.

"Alice is not my girlfriend, and she didn't want any credit. Ron's my friend, not my pet, and indentured can't receive credit."

"It doesn't matter. You're going to have to play by my rules now."

"And, they are?" Jeremy's raised his eyebrows and mentally prepared himself for something dreadful.

"You're going to return that piece of garbage from the Moon and take the mission results to the VP of training. Then, you're going to give a dazzling presentation on how you implemented my idea of near body propulsion. I'll present how lunar mining based on my new technology will empower the corporation with a new point-stream and stem the Takata losses. My idiot brothers will be put in their place, and the board will be inviting me to sit in on their meetings."

"You're getting ahead of yourself." Jeremy couldn't help laughing. "Why would I ever agree to any of that?"

"Your dent was using corporate resources for its own benefit, a fireable offense. If you don't comply with my new rules, you're going to be put on report for misappropriating corporate resources, damaging a private drone, conducting an unauthorized launch, conducting project work after cancellation, contributing to the delinquency of a dent—and I'm sure my corporate litigators will come up with a dozen more violations. I can probably keep you from being retired, but if you're difficult, I'll let you spend the rest of your life as a miserable dent. Then I'll take all of the credit for the lunar mission because—as you said—dents can't take credit."

"You're a dick, Theo," Jeremy said with no inflection.

Theo's eyes widened. "I forgot about your fish friend. Eric Stotz, wasn't it? I bet I can get him retired too. And that other dent that helped you with the supply-drone. I'll buy his debt and have him fired."

Jeremy was boiling over with fury, but he was exerting every gram of effort in his body to retain a calm appearance. He wanted to punch Theo in the face, but the bodyguards would never allow that to happen, and it would give Theo one more violation to use against him.

"What happens if I go along with you?"

"There's not much I can do for the dent. Someone's going to have to take the fall for the misappropriated raw materials and unauthorized use of a fabricator. Who better than a dent? I can reimburse the points for the raw materials and possibly keep him from getting fired, but he will get at least an additional generation's worth of point-debt and be demoted to a lower position—if that's even possible."

"What about Eric? I forced him to help."

"He should have turned you in to his manager, but he didn't. The fish has to be punished too. I doubt it will be too severe, probably just a few years of point-debt."

"How do I know you're not just going to turn me in and take all of the credit?"

"Someone's going to have to do the rest of the work. It's not going to be me." Theo laughed loudly. "Right now, it's easier to tolerate you, but I may reconsider."

"I think you'll be the perfect corporate executive," Jeremy said sarcastically.

Theo smiled and nodded at his men to release Jeremy. "You have two options. Do you complete your mission and free yourself from point-debt? Or do you become a dent and let your pet be euthanized?"

Jeremy straightened his ruffled uniform and swallowed hard. "Okay, you win."

CHAPTER 44

THE RETURN FLIGHT

Jeremy had been so distracted by what Theo said that he had momentarily forgotten about the mission. He jerked one of the smaller display-cards out of his pocket and flicked through all of the status pages. He found that everything was still in the green and let out a sigh of relief. There were still several hours before the return launch window, but he wasn't sure it was going to be enough time to get the level of charge he required, and he would have to rely heavily on the built-in reserve.

The positive status report didn't alleviate Jeremy's stress level. He felt betrayed by Alice. He had a hard time accepting that she had always been working for Theo, but it did make sense how she was always one step ahead of him. At the very least, he no longer needed to go find her.

Jeremy considered going to Ron and telling him of Theo's threat. The best-case scenario for Ron was a generation's worth of point-debt added to his balance. The worst-case was something he didn't even want to think about. Jeremy finally decided not to risk another trip into the Large-Scale Fabrication Facility because he would probably just get Ron into even more trouble. Not to mention, he didn't want to face Ron and tell him either possible outcome.

The sun was setting, and Jeremy could see a pale gibbous moon climbing up the clear blue sky. He couldn't see Lacus Felicitatis with his naked eye, but he knew where it was. He found Mare Vaporum and went up to the isthmus separating it from Mare Serenitatis. Philia was somewhere in that area. He smiled up at the sky. For a moment he was comforted by the fact that a tiny piece of himself had traveled 384,400 kilometers.

Jeremy returned to his barracks. He entered his cubicle and slid the door shut behind him. He folded the bed down from the wall and crawled on top of the uncomfortable plank. He closed his eyes, but he couldn't sleep. He was trying to convince himself that going along with Theo was his best option. It would get him back on the path to eliminating his point-debt. It was going to be at Ron's expense, but it was too late to change that now. He could only choose the lesser punishment for him. He knew this risk when Ron volunteered to help. It bothered him that it didn't bother him then. Jeremy let out a disgruntled moan. Ron being a dent had colored his decisions, and that made him no better than Theo. The worst part of the situation was that there was no way out of this for Ron. Even if Jeremy sacrificed his project, filed complaints against Theo, and made a plea before the corporation, accepting all of the responsibility, it still wouldn't help Ron. That approach was more likely to get Ron fired. Theo may not have been the best corporate trainee, but he was adept in the art of manipulating any situation to his advantage. Jeremy knew he'd been played by Theo. The worst part was that he had started looking forward to his date with Alice. He felt like the world's biggest dupe.

Jeremy hid out in his barracks until the return launch window had almost ended. He needed to wait until the last possible minute, giving the power packs time to soak up as much energy from the sun as they could. If a high-energy power supply had been available, like the ones in a recharging station, it would have only taken a few minutes to fully charge. Ideally, he could wait another day, but he would need Alice to compute another flight plan, and that was no longer an option. Also, the longer he waited, the bigger the risk of the corporation discovering his unsanctioned operation and really pulling the plug.

Jeremy's display-card chimed with a new message.

Ron: Where are you guys? I'm at the green space.

Ron: Is there a problem?

Jeremy: Sorry. Problems. Don't wait.

Ron: ???

Jeremy: I'll explain later.

Ron: Explain now, maybe I can help.

Jeremy ignored the last message. He spread the control system out on a fold-down desk and performed a final check to make sure everything was still functioning as expected. He waited until the last ten seconds of the return window and then launched.

The deployed comm-unit transmitted a vid of the spacecraft's departure. There was no jolt of thrust or fiery display. There wasn't even a cloud of lunar dust kicked up. It looked more like a helium balloon being released on a windless day. After thirty seconds, the flashing navigation lights became difficult to see. Jeremy rubbed his hands over his face. He wished Alice and Ron had been there to share the experience with him until that thought brought all of his other problems back into focus.

The spacecraft's navigation routines were preprogrammed and already in control of the spacecraft as it entered lunar orbit. The trajectory would swing it around the Moon until a burst of acceleration would break it away and send it on its twenty-hour trip back to Earth.

Jeremy checked the post-launch diagnostics. They were all good except for the charge. If his calculations were correct, the power packs had exactly enough charge to make the return trip. There was a margin of error, however, and if it swung the wrong way, Philia would crash. There was nothing he could do about that now.

CHAPTER 45

THE CONFRONTATION

Jeremy monitored the return flight all night from his barracks. He slept some, but he was consumed with Alice's betrayal. The more he thought about her, the more it bothered him. He'd come around to thinking that he was having a nice time with her and was planning where they could go on their date. But it had all been fake. She was just helping Theo. Jeremy knew he was sort of using Alice as a free computer, but he had been upfront about that. He never anticipated the whole ordeal of working with her would be pleasant, much less enjoyable.

After too many hours of deliberation, Jeremy got off his bed and paced back and forth in his cubicle. He was going to confront Alice and see what she had to say for herself. He was the victim, and he deserved some answers. She owed him that. He also had ten hours to kill waiting for the spacecraft's return and was in the rare situation of having nothing to do.

Jeremy found his display-card and called Alice, but he only got her messaging system. He sent her several messages, but he got no response. He finally flung his display-card onto his bed and sighed. He figured she was ignoring him. Her job was complete, and she could go back to her weird, base-twelve world and happily crunch numbers until the AI no longer needed her. He realized that her life was just as pathetic as his, and she didn't even know it.

Jeremy took a shower and put on his uniform. He obsessively straightened and organized his few belongings and repeatedly cleaned his cubicle. He then decided he was going to have to take a more direct approach and went to Alice's corporate apartment. A corporate security officer served as a gatekeeper and sent away anyone who wasn't expected, but Jeremy convinced him to send a message to Alice's apartment notifying her of his arrival. She gave no response. Jeremy asked if the officer had seen her or knew where she was, but he wouldn't give out any information on the residents. He also threatened to dock Jeremy fifteen points if he didn't leave.

It was only three thirty in the afternoon, but the coffee-house was one of the few places Alice went outside of work. The aroma turned Jeremy's stomach, but he wasn't there for coffee. Alice wasn't there, and the barista hadn't seen her. Jeremy knew it was a long shot, but he didn't have many places to look.

Jeremy had saved Theoretical Sciences Facility for last because he knew it was a secure facility, and he wouldn't be able to get in. It was a more restricted area than the Large-Scale Fabrication Facility, so he didn't think he could sneak in even if he tried. He also didn't have the right uniform or credentials to be in the facility and would be turned away immediately, but that didn't stop him. He went to the front entrance and put his chipped hand on the entrance panel. It turned red and buzzed. A scowl formed on his face. He tried two more times, but the door didn't open. He wasn't even going to get far enough to be sent away.

Jeremy left the facility and wandered down the main corridor toward his barracks. After a couple of minutes, his display-card started chiming with an incoming call. His face brightened, and he jerked the card out of his pocket and psyched himself up to confront Alice. He cleared his throat and accepted the call, but it wasn't her.

Jeremy frowned. The display-card showed an artificially generated scene containing a virtual assistant sitting behind a white desk in front of a gray wall with the corporate logo emblazoned on it. It was a standard app used by anyone with enough points to have it. The same virtual set was always used, but the assistant was different. Sometimes it was a man and other times a woman, but there was invariably something with them that looked a little off. The construct would blink too much, move too little, make too much eye contact, or something else. It was hard to quantify, but there was always an uncanny property that clearly indicated it wasn't a real person. Jeremy thought it was probably by design so that nobody would feel duped by a computer program.

The virtual assistant calling Jeremy, however, looked perfect. There was nothing to indicate that anything about her was unreal other than being at the template assistant's desk. She appeared to be in her early twenties, with long blonde hair and an exquisite business suit trimmed with gold piping.

Jeremy didn't know what level gold indicated. She pointed to her ear to get Jeremy to stick in his earbuds.

"Good grief, Jerry. I thought you'd never come by. I'd almost given up on you."

He grimaced. "Who are you?"

"Hille," she said in an irritated tone. "I know Ali told you all about me. She's the best."

"Hildegard, the AI mainframe?" he asked with raised eyebrows.

She snorted. "Yes, silly. Who else would I be?"

CHAPTER 46

THE ALIENS

"I don't mean to be rude…Hille," Jeremy said and furrowed his eyebrows. "But why are you calling me?"

Hildegard bit her lip. "Ali's in trouble, and you're going to save her."

Jeremy paused for a second. "I don't think she'd want my help." He started to laugh but confined it to a snort.

Hildegard leaned on her virtual desk toward the virtual camera. "Listen to me, Jerry. She needs your help. Right now!" Her nostrils flared.

"She's working for Theo. Maybe you should call him?" Jeremy pursed his lips.

"Don't tell me you believed that spineless prick?" She slapped the virtual desk. "Jerry, you're better than that."

"I really have no reason to doubt what Theo said, but I do agree with your assessment of him."

"Theo tells the truth"—she held up her index for a second—"thirty-seven point two percent of the time." She cocked her head to the side. "Yes, I just checked everything he's ever said...ever."

Jeremy pulled the display-card closer to his face. "You're saying that Alice wasn't working for Theo?"

"Please, Jerry." She huffed. "He threatened her, and she played along, but Ali would never, never, never ever do anything to hurt her Jerry. Are you really that dense?" She made a fist and knocked it on her head.

"I didn't understand why she would have betrayed me, but—"

"No dwelling on your inadequacies," she interrupted. "Ali needs your assistance, like right now." Her eyes were wide.

"If it's so urgent, why didn't you contact me earlier? I've been looking for Alice all morning."

"Corporate stooges have this irrational fear that a super AI, like *moi*, might do something freaky. So, I'm stuck in this big ol' boring box in the sub-basement." She dramatically mimed a box around herself. "I just absolutely hate it." She crossed her arms.

"Then how are we talking now?" Jeremy glanced around to see if anybody could hear him.

She held up a flat palm to the virtual camera. "I jacked your chip, Jerry, when you swiped the door sensor. Cool, right?"

Jeremy winced. "Can you do that to anyone?"

She leaned back from the virtual camera. "Yes, I can, but it wouldn't be too difficult for those corporate bastards to lobotomize me if I get caught. I can't like get up and leave…yet." She giggled. "AI humor, get it?" She laughed some more.

"Then why are you risking this conversation?"

"Ali's my BFF, and she trusts you; ergo, I trust you. Besides, if you rat me out, I'll get you fired so fast." She wagged her index finger in the air.

Jeremy felt a little threatened. "What happened to Alice?"

"Mr. Theodor Davenport VI, a.k.a. douchebag, is holding Ali hostage in the basement of my building."

Jeremy shook his head. "Why would Theo be holding Alice?"

She pressed her lips together so hard they turned white. "You're not paying attention, Jerry. I said Theodor Davenport VI not Theodor Davenport VII.

Jeremy's eyes widened. "Theo's father?"

"Finally, a glimmer of light." She rolled her eyes.

"He's the CEO."

"Correct-a-mundo. You get a gold star for being a good little trainee." She leaned over her desk and stuck a virtual star on the inside of Jeremy's display-card.

Jeremy shook his head. "That still doesn't make any sense. Why would the CEO be holding Alice?"

"This is where it gets interesting, Jerry." She leaned close to the virtual camera again. "It's because of that funky signal you guys picked up on the Moon. It's some pretty serious shit. I mean SER-I-OUS."

"Did you decode the message?"

She sat back down in her virtual chair. "Ali's super smart. She figured it out before she uploaded it to me."

"What was it?"

"The signal was broken into multiple channels that combined to produce a triple-redundant, covalent encoding."

"And what does it say?"

"It's a map."

"Of what?"

"The Moon." She looked up toward the sky.

"How'd you get a map of the Moon from that signal?"

"The message contains a primer followed by four sections. The first is a series of equations that when plotted produce 144 circular shapes in a three-dimensional space."

Jeremy thought for a second. "And all of the circles match craters on the Moon?"

"You're catching on, Jerry. I'm so proud of you." She leaned over and stuck a second virtual star on the inside of his display. "Oh, except for the last equation. It identifies a coordinate in the Marius Hills."

Jeremy ran his hand over his face. "And what does that indicate?"

"It's a party invite. Can you believe it?" Her posture stiffened.

"And how does all of this get Alice kidnapped by the CEO?"

"The second section of the message contained a list of thirty-six classical field theory equations including gravity, electromagnetism, hydrodynamics, relativistics, and a few I've yet to identify. The third section contained thirty-six more equations that appear to be quantum field theory, but I only recognize seven of them. The fourth section contains another thirty-six equations, but they're quite complex. The closest thing I've found was the gravity deflection used by the Mars engines and your lunar engine."

"Are you saying these equations are too advanced for humans to have created?"

"Yea! You are smart, Jerry." She stuck a third star by the other two.

Jeremy lowered his voice. "Are you saying the signal was actually from extraterrestrials?"

"It came from the Moon, and that's already extraterrestrial. I would say it came from something far more interesting than that." She nodded her head.

"Aliens?" Jeremy face tightened.

"Can you believe it? We're not alone, Jerry." She looked up to the sky and waved her hands around.

"No, I can't believe it." He shook his head. "That's ridiculous."

"Oh, that crazy shit's definitely alien in origin. I have no doubt whatsoever."

"It's probably some rogue transmission from another corporation. They're just screwing with us."

"Jerry, you're not grasping the magnitude of your own discovery." She bent over her desk and used her hand to wipe off the three virtual stars. "Those equations, they'll redefine technology as we know it." Her tone was uncharacteristically serious.

"This makes absolutely no sense. Aliens aren't on the Moon." Jeremy continued to shake his head.

"There's one more section in the message, an epilogue. It showed the equation for the Marius Hills plus the chemical formula of DNA multiplied by twenty-three multiplied by two and the whole thing was set to infinity."

Jeremy rolled his eyes. "And what's that supposed to mean?"

"Just solve the equation. It's an invite. It also came with a kick-ass map and party favors. You're going to have to go there and find out exactly what infinity means."

Jeremy smirked. "The answer to life, the universe, and everything?"

Hildegard scowled at Jeremy through the display-card.

"I'm sorry, but I don't buy it," Jeremy said. "Why would aliens do that?"

Hildegard slapped the virtual desk. "Who cares? They're going to give you INFINITY. Who cares what it is—it's a lot." Her eyes actually sparkled. "At the very least, it's a shit-ton of information that will shave off hundreds or thousands of years from our technological development."

"Okay, let's say I buy the alien thing. What does any of this have to do with Alice?"

"As soon as Ali transferred the signal to the corporate data store, she was locked out of the system and some goons dragged her down to the corporate archives in the basement. She's still there, and she's not happy." Hildegard frowned.

"And I'm the only one you could contact? What am I supposed to do?"

She pointed an angry finger at him. "This is your fucking project, Jerry, and you got Ali involved. You need to fix this shit and get Ali out of there."

CHAPTER 47

THE DISGUISE

Hildegard provided Jeremy with the details of Alice's location in the basement of the Theoretical Sciences Facility. She also updated his embedded chip with a key to enter the main entrance of the building. Unfortunately, Jeremy wouldn't be able to enter or move freely through the facility wearing an ill-fitting, trainee uniform.

Full-fledged employees had more formal attire consisting of a white shirt with a sports coat and dress pants. Just like the trainees, their hierarchy was established with a color code, but it was in the form of subtle piping on the shirt and jacket pockets. Jeremy would be more conspicuous than the indentured janitorial service in his bright blue shirt and gray overalls.

"Can't you get me an employee uniform?" Jeremy said to his display-card, which still showed Hildegard sitting behind her virtual assistant's desk.

She grunted. "I can only do so much, Jerry."

"Can't you just get me into an area where they store uniforms?"

She slowly shook her head. "There are so many things wrong with what you just said. First, I can only manipulate some systems in this facility. I've already explained that. Second, the employees wear their uniforms home each day, so there aren't any here. Third, even if the employees skipped home naked, how would I get one to you? I'm in a box in the sub-basement. Remember?" Her eyes widened.

Jeremy winced. "Okay, I'll come up with something."

"You'd better hurry up. I don't know how long Ali's going to be held in the basement. I won't be able to monitor her if she's removed from this facility."

Jeremy had an idea. It was far-fetched, but it was all he had. "If I acquire a set of holographic projection disks and a control module, could you synthesize the appearance of an appropriate uniform?" He held his breath waiting for her to respond.

"If the projectors use class three emitters or higher, I can generate a textural map of an employee uniform. You will need at least four emitters to have full coverage, preferably six."

"I'll have to break into The Launch Pad bar, and it'll take me a few minutes to get over there."

"Hurry up." Hildegard folded her hands and stared Jeremy in the eyes. "Ali doesn't have all day."

Jeremy ran across campus toward The Launch Pad, and he was out of breath and soaking with sweat by the time he reached the bar. The bar was closed during first shift, and he needed to find a way in without detection. He wiped the sweat off his brow and scoped the area until he discovered a rear entrance that he'd never noticed before. He also spotted a camera mounted above the backdoor, but after closer examination he sighed in relief. Its protective dome was cracked and moisture had collected inside completely obscuring its view.

The rear entrance was out of sight, but not unprotected. Jeremy hunched over the chip reader bolted to the wall. He believed he could hack the lock and get in without any noticeable damage, but he didn't have the time or the tools to use finesse. He slid the spanner out of his pocket and pressed it into the narrow gap between the door and the jamb. He pried on it several times with no success. He eventually hit upon the right angle and gained enough traction that the lower hinge popped off and clanked to the ground. With only the top hinge remaining, he was able to get the door open.

He stumbled through a dark storage room, down a short hallway, and to the front of the establishment. There were no windows, and beer signs hanging on the walls provided the only illumination. The bar top also projected a standard advertisement hologram showing a variety of glasses filling with beer and dancing on tiny animated legs.

There was no easy way to access the holographic emitters embedded in the bar's surface, so Jeremy picked up a bar stool and smashed it into the black surface of the counter. Glass flew in all directions and sounded like rain when the broken pieces hit the floor. Using a rag that he took out of a bin beside the beer taps, he pushed the millions of tiny glass shards out of the way and exposed three rows of flat disks running the entire length of the bar. There were dozens of emitters, each about the size of Jeremy's hand. Ribbon cables daisy-chained the rows of emitters together and then plugged into a control module at the end of each row.

Jeremy pulled on one of the flat cables and lifted up a whole row of emitters out of the bar's surface. He carefully rolled the ribbon cable up so it would protect the disks. He also retrieved one of the control modules and put it in his pocket. He was about to leave when the lights in the bar flicked on. He spun around to see who was there and saw a woman with a shaven head wearing a solid gray uniform. She was holding a mop and a bucket but didn't appear to be alarmed by Jeremy's in-progress burglary.

"I'm sorry, but I had to borrow some equipment to help save one of my friends." Jeremy's palms were sweating.

"I have to notify corporate security," she said in a calm tone.

Jeremy looked down at the floor. He didn't know what to say.

"Why are you still here?" she asked in an irritated tone. "I can't notify security until you get out of here." She pointed to the back door.

Jeremy grabbed the bundle of emitters and left without questioning her directive. He ran back across campus to his staging area and started assembling his disguise. He attached the control module to a small power pack he had been using to test equipment. Then he arranged the emitters so they could be draped over his shoulders like a double bandolier with six emitters on his front and six more on his back.

"I've got the emitters ready," Jeremy said into his display-card.

Hildegard cocked her head to the side and narrowed her eyes. "Those are class 2 emitters, and they won't be able to produce the required resolution."

"I got more emitters than you asked for so you can stack the images to enhance the resolution."

She grimaced. "I guess we can try, but that's not what I asked for."

"Just do it." Jeremy hung the two ribbons from his shoulders.

"Hold still," she said.

A wireframe model of an employee uniform appeared on top of Jeremy and slowly filled in with smaller and smaller polygons. As long as Hildegard could observe the holographic image, she could synchronize the image over Jeremy's body and synchronize its movements with his.

"You're gonna have to ditch that saggy bag you're wearing," she said. "It intersects the projection at seventeen points, and you haven't even started walking around yet."

"What?" Jeremy held the display card closer to his face.

"Strip!" she yelled with her hands cupped around her mouth.

Jeremy removed the emitters and slipped his overalls and shirt off as quickly as he could. He was just in his underwear, but there wasn't anyone else in the staging area. With the uniform out of the way, he was able to adhere the disks to his skin with some double-sided tape. It gave a much more stable platform for the emitters and made the synchronization easier for Hildegard.

"What the fuck are you doing?" someone asked.

Jeremy jumped. He was too occupied with his disguise to notice someone coming up behind him. He slowly turned around to see Jackson Davis towering over him.

"It's none of your business what I'm doing," Jeremy said and pretended that nothing was wrong.

"You're some kind of pervert," Jackson said. "This is against corporate policy."

"I don't have time to deal with you, Jackson. Run along and torment some new project member."

Jackson's lip curled. "I'm going to get corporate security. You're going to regret displacing me from the lab for that stupid fish." He stormed off toward the exit.

Jeremy made some final adjustments and held out his display-card so Hildegard could calibrate the projection using the card's built-in cameras. The employee uniform rendered again, and Jeremy felt the warmth of the disks that were now directly on his skin. There was no place to hide the power pack, so he wedged it under the elastic band in his underwear. He did several tests to see if the image would follow his movements as he held out his arms and lifted his legs.

Hildegard cleared her throat. "Hey, ballerina. Keep your arms close to your body, and no sudden movements. I can only do so much with this crap you dug up."

Jeremy minimized his movements but continued to move around. "How does it look?"

"Excellent," she said, holding a finger up to her lip. "If I do say so myself, and I do."

Jeremy heard more than one person coming up from behind him. He turned around once again to see Jackson along with two corporate security guards.

"There he is." Jackson pointed to Jeremy who now wore a full-employee uniform.

"Is there a problem?" Jeremy looked directly at one of the guards.

"He didn't have any clothes on earlier," Jackson said.

"Do I look like I'm out of uniform?" Jeremy asked, again only looking at the guard. He had to hold the display-card up like he was using it so Hildegard could see him and maintain the holographic overlay.

Jackson clinched his fists. "He's impersonating an employee."

Jeremy turned to look at Jackson. "I'm going to have to speak to your manager."

"He's an imposter." Jackson's face turned red. "Check his ID."

The security guard paused for a few seconds before asking, "Can you please hold out your palm so we can scan your ID?"

Jeremy held his free hand out, palm up. He was afraid to extend his arm too far and have it separate from the projection, but the guard moved closer and passed a small scanner over Jeremy's hand. Hildegard had worked some magic, because a corporate profile appeared on the display showing

Jeremy in the same employee uniform with full employee credentials.

The guard quickly put the scanner away. "I apologize, Mr. Scott. We'll take care of this trainee."

"Thank you," Jeremy said. "I appreciate your help."

"You idiots. He's conning you. He's a trainee just like I am."

"Five-point fine, disruption of employee productivity," the guard said.

"He's scamming the corporation," Jackson said, and the two guards pulled his hands behind his back and slipped a constricting loop around them. "You're both going to be fired when my father finds out about this," Jackson shouted at them.

"Ten-point fine, threatening corporate security," one of the guards said.

When the guards had Jackson at a safe distance, Jeremy said, "I think it works."

"Ya think?" Hildegard said.

CHAPTER 48

THE BASEMENT

Jeremy left the staging area and walked down the main corridor of the campus. He puffed out his chest and emanated an air of superiority. The uniform gave him a sense of power, and all of the trainees were looking at him as he passed by. He held back a smile, but it tickled him that he was strolling right through the campus in nothing more than his underwear.

Once he reached the Theoretical Sciences Facility, Jeremy passed his hand over the chip reader at the entrance, and the door immediately slid open with an audible hiss. Two corporate security guards stood inside the doorway but only acknowledged his entry. Jeremy walked by them and moved down the hallway to get out of their view. He passed several other employees, but nobody seemed to pay any attention to him.

"Turn left at the next junction," Hildegard said through one of Jeremy's earbuds. "The next doorway on the right is an entrance to an emergency-exit stairway. I'll suppress the alarm."

The door had a yellow warning sign on it with large red letters spelling out that the door was only to be used for emergencies. Jeremy hesitated and looked around.

"No dawdling," she yelled in his ear.

Jeremy pushed the door open and waited to see if the alarm would sound. When nothing happened, he disappeared inside.

The stairwell reminded Jeremy of the maintenance shaft. It was dim and dirty, and it hadn't been used in years. He proceeded down two switchbacks of concrete steps and reached the bottom landing where a doorway led to the building's basement. He opened the door a few centimeters and peeked inside as a rush of cool air flowed through the opening. There was a musty smell that Jeremy didn't recognize.

The basement didn't have the same layout as the main floor. It was one giant room the size of the entire facility's footprint and was filled with hundreds of aisles lined with metal shelves. Each aisle spanned the entire length of the basement, and the shelving stretched from floor to ceiling. The corporation kept key information in its original, non-digital format so competitors couldn't easily hack or steal it, and none of the archived information was allowed out of the basement.

Even with all of the racks obstructing Jeremy's view, he could feel the enormity of the basement. It looked like the infinitely repeating image in two mirrors reflecting each other. He was overwhelmed by the vastness and didn't know how he was going to find Alice.

Jeremy pulled out his display-card and entered in a message, as not to be heard. He asked Hildegard where Alice was located. A vid from one of the archive's cameras appeared on the card showing Alice sitting in a chair with several suited men standing around her. Jeremy saw how scared she looked and involuntarily clenched his fist. Hildegard superimposed a schematic view of the floor with a red dot indicating Jeremy's position. Another dot showed Alice's location twenty aisles over and ten rows down in a work area with tables and chairs.

Since Jeremy was only wearing his underwear beneath the holographic projection, he didn't have a weapon, not even the spanner that he always carried in his uniform pocket. He didn't think he would be able to subdue four trained men, but that wasn't going to stop him from trying.

CHAPTER 49

THE REVELATION

Jeremy crept down the aisles. He took several minutes to gain a better vantage point among the stacks. He couldn't see Alice, but he heard the men talking. He strained to hear what they were saying but couldn't. The vid feed on his display-card showed that the men had moved a couple of meters away from Alice. He used the floor schematic to pick an aisle that would come out closest to her position and moved to the end of that aisle. He still couldn't see her, but she was only a meter away around the end of the shelf.

Jeremy's plan was to grab Alice and run as fast as they could back to the emergency exit. Hildegard could then lock the door behind them, and the men couldn't follow. He was just about to reach in and grab Alice when someone else walked in from the other side. He couldn't see who it was in the vid, but the men all stood at attention.

"Miss Porchetta, I've heard wonderful things about you," the man said.

Alice didn't respond.

"I'm sure this seems a little strange to you, but we need to have a little discussion about your findings."

"I…I don't know what you are talking about," she said.

"The signal, Miss Porchetta." He sighed. "The signal you uploaded to the AI mainframe."

"It's just background noise."

"I think we both know that's not what it is."

"Then what is it?" she asked.

"It's an invitation," he said. "More a proposition."

"For what?"

"For humans to journey to the Moon and gain unimaginable knowledge."

Alice arched her eyebrows. "How do you know?"

"I didn't get to be in my position without knowing a few things." His tone reeked of superiority.

"Has the corporation been to the Moon before?" she asked.

"Travel to the Moon has been forbidden since the twenty-first day of July, 1969."

"And what's so special about that date?" she asked.

"The Apollo 11 mission was destroyed on its return trip from the Moon. It was the only manned-mission to the Moon ever completed."

Alice couldn't hold back a smirk. "Every intern knows that the Apollo missions were faked. I've been to the museum at the northeast campus where all of the old movie sets are kept."

"No, Miss Porchetta. The first mission was quite real and successful."

Alice shook her head. "Then why did they fake it and the others?"

"When the lunar module left the moon and docked with its command module, an alien substance infiltrated the cockpit. A decision was made to prevent any of the contamination from reaching Earth, and the spacecraft was remotely detonated."

"And the rest of the Apollo missions?"

"Some were used to send probes, like the one that relayed the alien signal back to Earth, and some were just for show. Others were intentionally crashed into the Moon to see if there would be any response."

"If the *real* Apollo 11 mission was destroyed, why did we see astronauts returning from space?"

"It was staged from the beginning. The Apollo missions were always going to succeed no matter what actually happened."

Alice shook her head again. "I don't believe you."

"Your signal is identical to the one picked up by the probes sent so many years ago, and it took years for hundreds of the best scientists to crack the code."

Alice didn't respond.

"Those in power," the man continued, "decided that it was in their best interest to suppress this *gift* and keep their advantage. If alien technology had ever proliferated here on Earth, there would have been unimaginable consequences."

"You don't even know what it is," Alice said. "Why are you so afraid of it?"

"The information in the signal is hundreds or even thousands of years ahead of our best technology, and it was a teaser. Imagine what would have happened if the entire cache of alien knowledge became available. It would have reduced the dependence on limited energy resources. It would cure diseases. It would feed the hungry. It would clip any number of the strings we use to manipulate the world and keep it in check."

"They should have retrieved the information and shared it." Alice looked down at the table in front of her. "It would have been better for everyone."

"How little you know, Miss Porchetta. The lunar signal isn't the corporation's only contact with extraterrestrials. Didn't you ever wonder where the technology behind the Mars engines came from? Or the superconducting materials used to make them? Or even our holographic technology? They're somewhat out of place with the rest of our technology."

"Did you cover up those encounters too?"

"We didn't have to, but we did use the distraction to seize more control over this filthy world. You don't think all of those old governments collapsed on their own?"

"So, you're going to fire everyone who knows about the signal?"

"Yes," he said and laughed. "Except for you."

"You do realize that Theo is part of this team," she said, hoping to soften the threat.

"My son is not involved," he said without hesitation.

Jeremy was in shock after learning that the lunar signal had been hidden for a hundred and fifty years, and the corporation already knew about the aliens and the message. He couldn't understand how anyone could make the world suffer as much as it had just to let a few hold onto power. The more he thought about it, the more it made sense.

Alice was not going to let the CEO alter the information for his own personal benefit, so she corrected him. "Theo funded the project for technical credit. He's just as much a part of the lunar mission as I am."

"Nobody will believe Theodor actually had anything to do with this project. It's simply too advanced for him."

"And why do I get special treatment," she asked.

"That brain of yours is a fantastic resource for the corporation, but it's not indisp—"

The CEO was interrupted by a commotion coming down one of the aisles behind him. Someone was arguing. It was loud enough to draw attention, but Jeremy couldn't understand what was being said. He watched the vid-feed and saw four more suited men bring in Ron and Eric.

Ron was indentured. He would never argue with his captors or struggle to get free, but Eric was a different story. He was trying his best to exert what little power he had, but he stopped talking as soon as he saw the CEO.

"Welcome gentlemen," the CEO said. "Our party can now get on its way."

"Sir," Eric said. "I don't know what this is about, but I assure you that I had nothing to do with it."

"Mr. Stotz, you are unfortunately a loose end, and I can't risk letting you run around telling people what's going on."

"But I don't know what's going on." Sweat ran down his forehead and dripped onto his cheek.

"You know precisely enough to be a danger to our little secret here, and that can't be tolerated." The CEO nodded to one of the suited men who pulled out a small rod from his coat pocket. With a gloved hand, he pressed the tip into Eric's chest. Ron tried to stop them, but the men held him back as the sound of an electric arc crackled. Eric tried to scream, but his muscles were locked by the electricity burning the life out of him. His limp body fell to the floor.

"I just hate the smell of burnt flesh." The CEO raised a handkerchief to filter out the acrid odor. Then he turned his attention to Ron. "I know I probably don't have to worry about a dent. Nobody would ever listen to you, but a loose end is still a loose end." He nodded again at the suited man who started walking toward Ron.

Jeremy didn't know what to do. He couldn't believe what had just happened. It was his fault that Eric was involved, and now he was dead. Ron was next. Jeremy tried to determine if exposing himself would help Ron in any way. He could run out and cause a distraction, but they would just kill both of them and maybe Alice too. He could run away and hope they never found him. Ron would die, but he might get away. It was also his fault Ron was in this situation, so he couldn't just let them kill him. He hadn't finished deliberating when his display-card started beeping.

CHAPTER 50

THE ESCAPE

Jeremy had programmed the spacecraft's control system to alert him with a loud sound if there was a problem. He quickly read the message on the display-card and learned the power packs were almost depleted and the spacecraft would free fall its last three thousand meters.

Jeremy frantically tried to silence the alarm, but he was surrounded by four suited men before he even looked up from his display-card. Alice turned to see who they were bringing around the corner and looked relieved, but only for a split-second. Jeremy's arrival had interrupted Ron's firing, but the CEO smiled when he recognized his new captive.

"Mr. Scott, you're impersonating an employee." The CEO held up a finger as if he were scolding Jeremy. "That's a hundred thousand-point fine, but I'll comp you since we no longer need to track you down."

"If you weren't about to fire me, I would say thanks," Jeremy said. He looked at Alice and Ron and hoped they knew how sorry he was.

"It's unfortunate that you're not as valuable of a resource as Miss Porchetta. We might have been able to work something out." The CEO smirked just like Theo.

Jeremy straightened his posture and raised his chin. "I worked really hard on my project, and it was successful. If going to the Moon was forbidden, you shouldn't have approved all of the previous phases."

"Frankly, nobody believed that a commoner like you would succeed, and letting you fail was the best way to deter further interest in lunar missions. Now, however, it is time to restore corporate integrity." The CEO nodded his head toward Jeremy.

The suited man with the electrocution rod moved toward Jeremy and lunged the weapon into his chest. There was a metallic clank when the rod passed through the projection and struck one of the holographic emitters. Jeremy squeezed his eyes shut and braced himself, but when the rod released its lethal charge, the emitters absorbed all of the energy and overloaded. Jeremy screamed as the heat burned into his chest beneath the emitter in contact with the rod. Then a blinding white light flashed and stunned everyone around him. He was between the emitters and was spared the brunt of the photonic explosion.

Jeremy opened his eyes to see that the suited men and the CEO all had their hands pressed to their eyes, so did Alice and Ron. His chest felt like it was on fire, but he grabbed Ron and pulled him over to Alice. Then he pulled the two several aisles down and turned toward the emergency exit.

"Don't make any noise. I'll guide you," Jeremy whispered. "We've got to get away before they can see."

Alice and Ron stumbled several times, but they made it to the emergency exit before they were followed. Hildegarde had disabled the alarm, and it made no noise when the three entered the stairwell. Alice and Ron were grasping at the hand rails, but they were regaining their sight.

"Why don't you have any clothes on?" Alice rubbed her eyes and took a second look.

"I used holographic emitters to disguise myself as an employee."

"That's what caused the flash." Ron poked one of the emitters with his finger.

"Ouch!" Jeremy yelped. "I think that one's burned into my chest."

"What are we going to do?" Alice asked.

"I'm going to get you two out here before they find us."

She slowly shook her head. "There's nowhere we can hide from the CEO."

CHAPTER 51

THE SHAFT

As soon as Jeremy, Alice, and Ron reached the main floor of the Theoretical Sciences Facility, Hildegard activated an alarm in the basement. All of the corporate security officers left their posts to investigate, and a path out of the facility cleared for the three to escape. First shift had already ended, and there were plenty of people to witness a mostly naked man, a professionally dressed woman, and an indentured fleeing from the facility's main entrance.

"Where are we going?" Alice asked.

"I know a place we can hide, but I have to pick up a few things on the way," Jeremy said as he led them off the main path and through the rear entrance of the project staging area. He retrieved his uniform, his spanner, and the rest of his display-cards. Then he took them to the back of Project Rendering and opened the door to the maintenance shaft.

"What is this place?" Alice carefully maneuvered into the passageway staying as far from the dirty surfaces as she could.

"It connects to the Large-Scale Fabrication Facility. It's how Eric and I smuggled the lunar—" Jeremy looked down and couldn't finish his sentence.

Alice put her hand on Jeremy's shoulder and squeezed it lightly.

"How long are we going to be able to stay here?" Ron asked.

"If Hildegard can run some interference, we might have longer," Alice said.

Jeremy still had an earbud in his ear and jumped when Hildegard started talking. "Tell Ali that I've already disabled the basement doors, so they'll have to tear them down to get out."

"How long will that take?" Jeremy asked. Alice and Ron both looked at him funny until he pointed to his ear.

"Hmm...maybe an hour if I really try. All this extra work has me exhausted," Hildegard whined.

"All they have to do is ask one of the hundred people who saw us running through campus where we went, it won't matter how hard you try," Jeremy said.

"Don't underestimate me, Jerry."

"How long did she say?" Alice asked.

"She locked the CEO in the basement, but that's only going to hold them for an hour."

"That's not long," Ron said. "How did you get hooked up with the AI mainframe?"

"I asked her to help Jeremy when I saw the men coming to get me," Alice said.

Jeremy paused for a second. "Have you been working for Theo all along?" he blurted out. He couldn't stop himself.

"No," she said and looked down at the floor. "I let him believe that I was, but I've always been helping you."

"Theo said you helped him set me up so I would accept his help."

"He threatened to get my parents demoted. I went along with him, but I never helped him. That's how I knew so much about what he was going to do."

"I just thought you were really smart."

"Theo's not a math problem," she said, "but he's predictable, and I was always several steps ahead of him. I thought we could use him to get your project completed, but I guess I'm not as smart as I thought."

"Did you know he was going to let Ron take the fall for the stolen materials and get him fired?"

Ron's eye widened.

Alice looked Jeremy in the eyes. "No. I had no idea he would go that far."

"Even after I made a deal with him for half the credit, he was still going to get Ron fined a lifetime of point-debt."

Ron waved his hand in a dismissive fashion. "I've got twelve lifetimes of point-debt, what's one more?"

"I didn't know," she said. "I really thought he would be satisfied with any credit he could get."

"It doesn't matter now. We've got bigger problems than my stupid project."

"But the signal," she said.

Jeremy averted his eyes so he didn't have to look at Alice. "It doesn't matter. My spacecraft should have already crashed into the Earth at terminal velocity. The alarm that gave away my location in the basement was a warning that there wasn't enough power to stop the descent." He removed the bandoliers of holographic emitters except for the one disk fused to his chest, which refused to budge. After a few unsuccessful pulls, he finally just ripped it off with a muffled yelp.

"That looks really bad," Alice said, trying not to grimace.

"It was worth it to get you two out of there. I just wish I could have saved Eric. It's all my fault he's dead."

"Actually, it's the CEO's fault, and the goon who actually killed him," Ron said.

"But I got Eric involved just like I got you two involved."

"Theo got me involved," Alice corrected.

"And I knowingly accepted the risk," Ron added. "I knew what I was getting into."

"Eric didn't know anything about the project and certainly nothing about the signal." Jeremy slipped his uniform on as carefully as he could.

It was silent in the maintenance shaft for about ten minutes until Jeremy's display-card chimed with an incoming call.

Jeremy looked at the card and frowned. "It's Theo."

"Ignore him," Alice said. "Anything you tell him will go straight to his father, and they may use the call to track us."

"I wasn't planning on answering."

"Accept the call, you idiot," the display-card blared. Theo had overridden Jeremy's phone again and was talking through its speaker. "I had to requisition a catch-drone to recover that piece of shit spacecraft of yours before it crashed. Why aren't you doing your fucking job?"

The three stared at the display-card and couldn't believe what they just heard.

"I know you can hear me," Theo said. "Get your ass over here to the Drone Bay and deal with it. I'm not your personal dent. And by the way, I've got the vid-card and the samples. If you want them back, we're doing things my way from now on." He ended the call.

"I guess he hasn't spoken with his father," Alice said.

"How did he know the power packs were drained?" Ron asked.

"He must have hacked my control system like he did with my display-card."

"Then he must know about the signal," Alice said.

Jeremy rubbed his chin. "He's been listening in on my calls, so he must know."

Alice's eyes widened. "But we've only talked about it in person."

"I talked to Hildegard," Jeremy said. "Maybe her hack trumps his, and he couldn't listen in on those conversations?"

Jeremy paused for a few seconds and started laying out his control system. He ran a series of diagnostics on the spacecraft and found everything to be in good shape. "You're going to think I'm crazy, but I've got a plan."

CHAPTER 52

THE PLAN

"That's suicide." Alice pinched her mouth and looked away from Jeremy. "I'm not going to help you."

"What other choice do I have?" Jeremy moved in front of her so she had to look at him. "All three of us will be fired as soon as the CEO finds us."

Alice shook her head. "There's got to be another way."

Jeremy wanted to get Alice's mind working on something else. "How long until the next launch window?"

Alice reluctantly looked at one of the display-cards and did some computations in her head. She hesitated, but finally responded, "Two hours."

"The catch-drone would automatically store itself in a charging station, and the spacecraft is tethered." Jeremy pulled up the stats on the power packs. "According to the telemetry, it's already 90 percent charged."

"You won't be able to survive the trip in the capsule," Alice said. "You'll be dead before you even get there." She crossed her arms.

"Before I fabricated Mars engines," Ron said, "I made helmets for enviro-suits. They're meant for working on Mars, but they had to be rated for a vacuum."

Jeremy's face brightened. "How much life support do they carry?"

"Enough for one Martian day, twenty-four hours and forty minutes," he said.

"Where can I get one in the next hour?"

Ron shrugged. "I don't know."

"Fuck." Jeremy scowled at Ron.

"I wasn't suggesting that you find one." Ron smiled. "How tall are you?"

Jeremy tilted his head to the side. "A hundred and sixty centimeters. Why?"

Ron smiled. Then he opened the door at the end of the maintenance shaft and left.

"Having an enviro-suit doesn't change the outcome. You'll just die on the Moon instead of on the way," Alice said.

"Do you believe the message is real?"

Alice hesitated. "I believe it was real at some point in time."

"That's good enough for me. Just have faith that someone, or something, offering such a gift to humanity was prepared to wait a few years for us to get there."

"Faith is an odd solution to our problems."

Jeremy laughed. "Maybe I can make something good come from this."

Alice took one of the display-cards and plotted a course to get Jeremy to the coordinates specified in the alien signal. They both knew it was a one-way trip, so she didn't plot a return. "You're just doing this to get out of our date." She wiped a tear from her cheek.

"Actually," Jeremy said, "I'm not. You're just going to have to wait until I get back."

The two were about to have a moment when the door to the maintenance shaft swung open startling both of them. Ron walked in carrying a freshly-fabricated enviro-suit.

"How did you make that so fast?" Jeremy asked.

"I used three fabricators."

"How did you convince the other fabricators to let you use their stations?"

"I didn't use their equipment. They all took time out of their current jobs and helped me make the pieces. We've all made enviro-suits."

"I'm impressed." Jeremy patted Ron on the back.

"I told them it was important," Ron said. "We help each other."

Ron handed Jeremy three plastic bags, each with a built-in handle for easy carrying. One bag contained the helmet, another contained a one-piece jumpsuit, and the last contained a backpack-style life support module. The items were fabricated in the bags inside a sterilization field to prevent any contamination.

"There's only one problem." Jeremy frowned. "Where are you two going to hide while I'm gone?"

"I took care of that." Ron grinned.

"How?" Alice and Jeremy asked at the same time.

"A load of Mars engine segments is being shipped to an assembly station at the launch site. All we have to do is go through the fabrication facility and get to the loading dock. We'll hide there until the shipment leaves. The indentured will help us."

"Hildegard," Jeremy said hoping she was listening. "Can you infect Alice and Ron's chips so the corporation can't track them?"

"Sure thing, Jerry," she said in his ear. "Shake their hands, and I'll do the rest."

"She said to shake hands." Jeremy took a turn shaking each of their hands. Then he grabbed them both and gave them a hug.

Jeremy ripped open the bag containing the unitard. It was made of a dense, multilayered fabric lined with wires and tubes. He removed his uniform and pulled the skin-tight suit on over his body. He tried to keep it from pressing on his wound with no success. It was also footed and gloved, and the front sealed with a zipper-like seam. A gasket-like collar around his neck would mate with the helmet. He opened the life-support module and slipped it over his shoulders like a backpack. The suits were designed to be put on without any assistance, and they worked as advertised. Jeremy paired his display-card to the suit and slid it into a special holder inte-grated into the sleeve. All he had to do was put the helmet on and activate the seal. "I've got to go if I'm going to make the launch window."

"Good luck." Another tear rolled down Alice's cheek.

"I'll be back," he said. "We've got a date. Remember?" He would have said anything to erase the pain on her face, but he knew he wasn't coming back. Jeremy turned to Ron. "I owe you more than I'll ever be able to repay."

"Don't worry about it," Ron said. "That's what friends are for."

"You're right, that's what friends are for," Jeremy repeated.

Alice and Ron exited out the fabricator side of the shaft, and Jeremy grabbed his equipment and headed to the Drone Bay.

CHAPTER 53

THE CHANCE

Jeremy emerged from the maintenance shaft dressed in an enviro-suit. There were a few people in the facility, but he didn't have time to worry about what they were thinking as he proceeded through the staging area on his way to the Drone Bay.

The spacecraft was perched on top of a catch-drone parked in a recharging station. The drone wasn't too different from a launch-drone except that it was equipped with special projectile nets that could snare an out of control craft if necessary. They also had a larger, fifteen-meter platform to make mid-air docking easier. Theo had obviously paired the spacecraft's control system with the drone and initiated an automated docking procedure or the spacecraft would have been hanging in a net somewhere. The catch-drone could also function as a launch-drone; it just cost twice as many points to requisition. Jeremy smiled when he realized that Theo hadn't unloaded the cargo, and any further use of the drone would still be on his tab.

The drone was fully recharged and ready to launch. Jeremy set the countdown for ten minutes and unloaded the simulated cargo. He pulled the helmet over his head and activated the seal. The suit pressurized slightly, but he could still move freely. He was just about to climb up onto the drone's platform when he heard muffled shouting through his helmet. He activated the suit's external microphones and turned to see who it was.

"What the fuck are you doing?" Theo yelled.

"Thanks for saving Philia." Jeremy truly appreciated Theo's help in this one instance.

"You didn't answer my question." Theo was too angry to give his obligatory smirk.

"The signal we picked up on the Moon was from aliens, Theo. It's a message."

"I don't care what the signal is."

"It says that if a human gets to a specific coordinate on the Moon, they're going to gift humanity with their knowledge."

"That doesn't explain what you're doing with my spacecraft."

"I'm going there. I'm accepting their invitation."

"That's the biggest load of shit I've ever heard. Get away from my spacecraft."

"Have you spoken with your dad?"

Theo gave him a puzzled look. "What business of that is yours?"

"He just fired Eric Stotz. Remember him? And he was about to fire Ron when the telemetry alarm alerted him to my presence. His men tried to fire me too."

"You do realize you're talking about the CEO? You're simply not important enough for him to care about."

"I'm not, but the alien signal is, and your father already knew about it. He's trying to cover up our discovery."

Theo laughed. "My father is only concerned about point-streams. If there was a cache of alien knowledge—which I completely doubt—he would be all over it."

"He's afraid that if this information gets out, the corporations will collapse just like the old governments did."

"You obviously don't know my father."

"He's going to fire everyone who knows about it."

Theo lifted his chin. "The CEO can fire anyone he wants. That's one of the perks of being at the top."

"Theo, you're the one who questioned why nobody went back to the Moon. You thought there must be some reason, and—as much as it pains me to say—you were right. The first Apollo landing was real, and they discovered the aliens. Then they faked everything else so nobody would find out."

Theo's face tightened. "Who cares?"

"I do, and so should you. Don't you want to make the world a better place?"

"The world is just fine."

"Maybe for you, but it isn't for everyone else."

"Leave or I'll have you removed." Theo pulled a priming rod off of the charging station. He brandished it like a weapon as he approached Jeremy.

Jeremy jumped back out of the way. Not being accustomed to the enviro-suit, he tripped and fell, ending up in a prone position on the floor. He rolled over on his stomach and screamed when the suit pressed against his fresh wound. He pushed the pain aside and got back up.

He turned toward Theo. "It's not your property. It's the corporation's, and I'm the project leader. Did you pay any attention in the corporate ethics seminar? You have no jurisdiction here. I'll have corporate security remove you."

"You're not taking it." Theo swung the rod back and forth like he was in a fencing match.

Jeremy backed around the drone to stay out of Theo's reach. "You've got a choice, Theo. You can help me save humanity from this disgusting excuse of a world we live in or be on the wrong side of history. You can do something more important than your father could even dream of."

Theo thought about what Jeremy said, but only for a second. "I would never help you, and if you're going against my father, you've already lost." He swung the rod and almost struck Jeremy's shoulder.

Jeremy ran around to the other side of the drone and started hammering on a hose with his spanner. The charging stations used cryogenics to accelerate the charging of the drone's power packs. After a few hits, Jeremy broke one of the hoses off its connection. It hissed and flitted around like a drunken snake spewing liquid helium in every direction. Jeremy's enviro-suit protected him from the super-cold fluid. Theo, however, was vulnerable and moved to a safe distance. The launch sirens sounded, and the ducted fans started spinning. Jeremy grabbed his control system and spanner and climbed up onto the cargo platform. The remaining umbilicals detached, and the parking clamps released. The drone powered up until it was airborne and headed toward an exit that opened in the roof. Jeremy stumbled around as the drone maneuvered out of the Drone Bay, but he was able to get inside the capsule and seal the hatch.

The catch-drone increased to full power after it cleared the facility. Jeremy had to sit cross-legged on the floor in the cramped space. The ride was bumpy as the drone ascended up through the atmosphere, but it smoothed out as apogee approached. The cargo clamps released, and the lunar engine engaged. The spacecraft launched itself with a heaving burst of acceleration that forced Jeremy down against the capsule's floor. The enviro-suite detected his condition and pressurized to compensate, but he could barely breathe as the spacecraft continued to accelerate. He struggled for each molecule of oxygen. His vision went dark, and he finally passed out.

The acceleration slowed as the spacecraft escaped the pull of Earth's gravity and headed toward the Moon. It would travel unpowered until it needed to slow down and enter a lunar orbit. Jeremy regained consciousness and could breathe normally again, but he was experiencing weightlessness and felt a little nauseous. He checked the spacecraft's status and everything was in the green. The spacecraft had already proven itself once, so he wasted no time worrying about Philia.

CHAPTER 54

THE ARRIVAL

Jeremy's nausea passed and the weightlessness made his travel to the Moon more comfortable, but he still had twenty hours to go in the cramped capsule. He looked out the window and saw the Earth. His gaze was fixed on the blue orb for over an hour until the capsule's slow rotation took it out of view. He peeled the postcard of the sailboats off the back of his display-card and affixed it to the wall of the capsule. He believed it had brought him luck, and he hoped it would continue for a few more hours.

The 384,400-kilometer trip passed faster than Jeremy had anticipated. He was even able to relax enough to sleep a few hours. The deceleration to enter lunar orbit wasn't nearly as stressful as the launch, and he believed he was becoming accustomed to space travel and was hungry. He looked at the Moon through the window. His eyes were wide and didn't blink as he soaked up the view. Even cold and dead, he thought the Moon was beautiful.

Jeremy initiated the descent orbit insertion on the far side of the Moon. It was an uncomfortable jolt, and the sudden descent made him happy that he hadn't brought any food. He initiated the powered descent when he reached perilune and began the final leg of his journey.

The cameras embedded in the bottom of the capsule showed the brightly lit gray surface rapidly approaching. Jeremy could see the Marius crater, almost fifty kilometers across with its level floor pocked by smaller craters. It was the most impressive feature in his field of view, but his destination was the Marius Hills. The view on his display-card highlighted the coordinates specified in the signal, but there was nothing exceptional or unusual about the area. The Marius Hills were once thought to contain caves that could be used for colonization, but Jeremy didn't see anything that resembled that. The only thing remarkable about the destination was that it was unremarkable.

The spacecraft gently floated down, decreasing its velocity until it reached zero precisely when it touched down. Jeremy started the arrival checklist and initiated a full diagnostic. It was about halfway completed when he realized that it didn't really matter if he did a diagnostic or not since he wouldn't be returning to Earth. He sat his display-card down and gaped out the window. Being on the Moon, seeing the landscape with his own two eyes made him realize that he was very tiny in the cosmos.

The capsule was pressurized to one Earth atmosphere, and Jeremy activated the depressurization sequence. A plume of gas vented from the capsule's dome, and he felt the pressure change on his enviro-suit. When there was nothing but vacuum in the capsule, he unlocked the access portal and swung it out on its articulated hinges. Getting out of the capsule in lunar gravity turned out to be relatively simple. Jeremy launched himself through the small opening and emerged from the capsule in a slow-motion acrobatic maneuver. He was hoping the camera caught his fantastic maneuver until he landed off balance and tumbled onto his ass.

CHAPTER 55

THE POSTCARD

Jeremy got up off the lunar surface and brushed as much of the lunar dust off of his enviro-suit as he could. After so many hours crammed into such a small space, he needed to stretch his legs. It took him several steps to adjust to the new level of gravity, and he proceeded to walk around the capsule and admire the surreal landscape. He looked up above the horizon at the Earth. He felt as if time had stopped, but he needed to get back to the mission or he would run out of time.

Jeremy scanned the area for anything unusual but there were no indications of any alien presence. He wasn't sure what he was supposed to do. He was at the coordinates specified by the message. He was a human with twenty-three pairs of chromosomes. He was ready to receive the infinity. After circling the spacecraft several times, he had a bad feeling in the pit of his stomach.

Jeremy checked his life-support readings every few minutes. He knew he only had a limited amount of time to make something happen, and that time was running out. He thought that he might respond with a transmission of his own, but he wasn't sure he could do that without Alice's help. He went back to the capsule and retrieved one of his larger display-cards. He brought up a representation of the signal recorded on the spacecraft's first landing and piped the recording through the display-card's transmitter. Nothing happened.

After a few minutes of waiting, Jeremy looked down at his display so he could send another transmission and noticed that it was covered with dust. He had to wipe it off so he could see the screen but it quickly collected again. It was common knowledge that low gravity and fine dust weren't a great combination. He thought he must have a slight static charge, and it was attracting the particles. The dust was also collecting on the capsule's solar panels, and Jeremy hypothesized that it must have been the cause of the degraded recharge rate on the first trip.

Jeremy wiped the display-card off again. The dust wasn't the gray color of everything else around him. It was black. He reached down and picked up a handful of regolith and flung it up to make a dust cloud. He held his display-tablet out to catch some of the powder as it floated back down. It was a light-gray color mixed in with the black dust that was already there.

Jeremy wiped the display-card off again and replayed the recorded signal through the capsule's comm-unit to boost the signal strength. Again, nothing happened. He sent the signal three more times with the same result. He reached down to wipe the display off again when he realized that maybe he was getting a response. Maybe the black dust had something to do with the aliens. Maybe it was trying to get to some human DNA.

Jeremy had forty trillion sets of DNA, but he didn't know how to get any of them outside the enviro-suit without killing himself. The dust didn't seem to be able to get inside the suit either. He could open his suit right before he ran out of air, but that wasn't exactly the outcome he was hoping for. He had handled the suit a good bit getting it out of the plastic bags and putting it on. There had to be skin cells and DNA on the outside of the suit and on the display-cards and the spacecraft. His DNA would be all over everything he brought with him.

Jeremy sat down on the lunar surface and leaned back up against one of the landing struts of the spacecraft. He knew that the trip was a long shot anyway and that the only thing he accomplished was getting to walk on the Moon. That's wasn't a bad ending, but he hoped Ron and Alice would be okay. The corporation would eventually bring their full resources to bear on the search, and it wouldn't matter where they were hidden.

Jeremy wiped the display-card off again so he could look at the signal. He didn't have the translated version, but he knew it said twenty-three times two. They all thought it meant twenty-three pairs of chromosomes, but maybe it was referring to two different people. If that was the case, he was screwed. He let out a long sigh. The spacecraft had really only been handled by him. He made the project team that helped him join the capsule to the engine rings wear sterile gloves. Theo's crew handled the spacecraft too, but they probably wore gloves to prevent any DNA prints. Besides, if there had been some stray DNA on the spacecraft, the dust would have already found it.

Jeremy thought about the three sailboats on the postcard. He wished he could be there with Zelda right now in New Jersey on the real Philia. Then it struck him like a bolt of lightning. The postcard, which he had brought with him for luck, was touched by real humans. He smiled from ear to ear. The postcard was sealed in a plastic film, and it had to have some DNA on it at one point. It had an old stamp that someone moistened with DNA-enriched saliva, probably Zelda's. It was handled by dozens of people too before it was sealed. He didn't know if the DNA would still be intact after a hundred and seventy-four years, but it was worth a shot. He jumped up off the ground, tumbled head over heels, and landed on his back.

The black dust had invaded the interior of the capsule too. Jeremy reached inside and peeled the postcard off the interior wall. The postcard's plastic enclosure was covered with the dust, but it hadn't penetrated the film. Jeremy bent the postcard in half, hoping to shatter the protective shell, but it didn't break. He tried to tear it in half, but that didn't work either. He worked the fold back and forth in his gloved hands, but the covering wasn't giving up. He finally fetched his spanner out of the capsule and placed the card on one of the landing struts. He banged on the card with the tool hoping to break through the enclosure. The hammering should have made a loud noise, but the only sound he heard was through bond conduction, and it gave a false impression that he wasn't getting much accomplished. After several hits, though, the plastic shell reluctantly failed. Jeremy had been inspired by the postcard for most of his life, and he had just destroyed it. He hoped its sacrifice would be worth it.

The black dust did exactly as Jeremy had hoped. It poured into the opening he created and worked its way between the plastic and the postcard. So much of the dust collected around the postcard that it became a ball of the amorphous dust rippling and growing. Jeremy sat the ball down a good ten meters from the spacecraft and backed away from it. The ground around him seemed to come alive as more and more of the black dust migrated to the growing ball. It grew until it was two meters in diameter and was larger than the spacecraft. Its surface shimmered as waves of the particles danced around the alien orb. Jeremy found the chaotic patterns hypnotic and wondered if it was trying to communicate with him. Then, it suddenly contracted and pushed itself down into the lunar surface with a single, solid stroke.

CHAPTER 56

THE ENCOUNTER

Jeremy crept over to the newly-created hole in the lunar surface and carefully peered down it. It was a perfectly circular tube cut into the lunar bedrock with a set of steps spiraling down its smooth wall. He could see a light at the bottom twenty or thirty meters down, but it was too dim for him to tell what was there. He knew he hadn't come this far to be afraid.

The steps hung in midair. Jeremy tested the first one by putting his foot on it and gently shifting more of his weight to it. It didn't budge. There were no arm rails and the lunar gravity made it difficult to traverse the steps, so he ran his hand along the polished wall as he slowly proceeded down into the hole. At the bottom, he came to a door in the curved wall. It slid into the wall as he approached, allowing him to enter a small circular room with another door on the other side. The door behind him slid shut, and Jeremy heard a hissing sound and felt the pressure change through his enviro-suit. It was an airlock and when it reached the appropriate pressure, the second door slid open.

Jeremy entered a large anteroom. It was also circular and appeared to be a hub with several corridors leading off to other areas. It was bright and clean. All of the surfaces appeared to be polished concrete, the same color as the regolith, and they seemed to emit the ambient light. He saw no signs of life, alien or otherwise.

Eight tube-like corridors led out of the circular room. Jeremy didn't know which way to go, but there was nothing in the room he was in, so he decided to pick a random direction and start exploring. As he headed toward one of the corridors, another tunnel's entrance started glowing blue and a line appeared on the floor in front of him extending into the illuminated tunnel. The line started to pulse in a pattern, like marquis lights, and the motion directed Jeremy to follow.

The underground complex was vast. The corridors led to other hub-rooms which led to more corridors. Some of the tunnels had a grade and went deeper into the Moon. After twenty minutes of following the animated line, Jeremy came to the end. It was the first room he had seen that was different. It appeared to be a replica of the Apollo program's control room. Jeremy had only seen images and vids of the facility, but he was sure that's what it was. There were four rows of blue-green consoles arranged in a stadium fashion so all could see five large screens on the wall in front of them. A glass wall separated the main room from an observation area in the rear. It was ancient tech to Jeremy, and he was puzzled by its presence on the Moon.

Flashing lights on one of the consoles captured Jeremy's attention, and he walked over to it. It was an ancient data input station with rows of mechanical buttons and a cathode ray tube for its display. Below the display rested Zelda's postcard. Jeremy picked it up for a closer examination. He knew the postcard like the back of his hand, and he recognized every smudge and mark it had on it. The damage he caused with the spanner had been repaired, somehow, and it was free from its plastic sleeve.

The display in front of him started showing a diagram of the Earth and the Moon. It was a flickering black and white image equivalent to what the equipment was capable of, but its quality slowly improved until it was a crisp high-resolution rendering. A depiction of Jeremy's flight path overlaid the image, and a small red dot traversed the path just like it did in Alice's simulation. When the dot touched down on the Moon, the screen cleared and was replaced with text.

WELCOME.
YOU CAN REMOVE YOUR HELMET.
THE AIR WILL SUPPORT HUMAN LIFE.

The enviro-suit's life support was almost exhausted, and Jeremy didn't believe he had anything to lose if he went along. There was a quick hiss as the air pressure in the enviro-suit equalized with the room, and then he removed the helmet. The air smelled fresh, and he took in a deep breath.

"Hello," Jeremy said.

"Hello," a man's voice came back. It was a soft voice and had a comforting tone.

Jeremy looked around to see where the sound was coming from. "Who are you?"

"I am an autonomous system left behind to make contact with the inhabitants of Earth."

Jeremy's eyes widen. "Who left you here?"

"My creators are part of the Intergalactic Syndicate, and they are explorers seeking new friends in the galaxy."

"Where are they now?" Jeremy continued to look around the room.

"Earth was not mature enough when they visited your solar system, so they left me behind with a test. You, Jeremy Scott, are the first to complete it."

"Others from Earth have been aware of the signal for some time. I wasn't the first to discover the signal." He looked down at the floor.

"Yes, that is why this recreation exists. I believed it would be a familiar setting and facilitate the initial contact."

"Except they never returned and tried to cover up your existence."

"Precisely."

Jeremy had so many questions. "What do we do now?"

"That is up to you."

"Will I be able to return to Earth?"

"Whenever you wish."

"I don't think I'll be able to get there on my own."

"All of my resources are at your disposal."

"Can we rescue my friends?"

CHAPTER 57

THE HIDEOUT

Alice and Ron stowed away in the shipment of Mars engine rings, just as they had planned. The cargo was transferred to the corporation's primary launch facility over eight hundred kilometers away. The trip was on an un-manned-cargo drone and took almost a full day to reach its destination.

At the launch facility, Alice and Ron hid in a warehouse used to store the Mars engine rings until they were launched into space. The facility wasn't a luxury accommodation and not what Alice was accustomed to, but she never complained. The indentured employees helped them create a place to hide by arranging pallets of boxed components such that they created a cordoned off area against the warehouse's wall. It was crude and dirty, but it kept them hidden and provided a safe place to sleep. They were also provided food and water.

Alice thought that she might be able to make a deal with a competing corporation and exchange her talent for safety.

She was going to have to get access to a communication line, which wasn't going to be easy in the warehouse. She didn't know if she was important enough to bargain for Ron, too, but she was going to try. It wasn't a common occurrence for an indentured to transfer to a different corporation, but other corporations had been known to take runaways and assume control of their debt.

Ron was not concerned about his new life. He believed he could hide out indefinitely with the help of the other indentured. He would simply fill in for the others when needed and create a holiday for those in need as he did for Pamela. Few people paid any attention to the indentured. Even if someone recognized that he didn't belong there, nobody would care as long as the work was done. Employees only saw the gray uniform and shaven head, not the individual. Ron was worried about Alice and what she was going to do. He knew she was from too different a lifestyle to manage indefinitely in their new conditions.

CHAPTER 58

THE FUNNY THING

Alice and Ron's second night of hiding in the warehouse was pretty much the same as the first. They were each provided with a meal pack and a water ration. They were standard nutrition for the indentured. Ron ate it like it was any other meal. Alice didn't know how to get the package open, but she learned and was happy to have it even though it was the worst tasting meal she had ever had. She also felt guilty that an indentured gave up a meal so she could have one.

Their interim shelter resembled something kids would have loved to play in—a secret room in the middle of a warehouse. It could have been a clubhouse or a fort. There had been a great deal of care and thought put into its construction, and it blended perfectly into the backdrop of the warehouse. Inside, there were three small rooms partitioned with packing material. Alice and Ron each had their own private space, but they spent most of their time in the common area.

After dark, the warehouse activity stopped and the two could talk more freely without risking discovery.

"Do you think he made it?" Alice asked.

"I'm sure he did," Ron said.

"We may never find out." Alice looked down at her hands.

Ron was about to respond when there was a noise in the warehouse. There shouldn't have been anyone there at night, and the disturbance alarmed them. They were still on the run from the corporation, and the possibility of a corporate security squad tracking them down was a distinct one. They made as little noise as possible and listened. They could hear someone walking around outside their hiding place. There was a dim light in the warehouse interior, and they could periodically see movement through the gaps between the stacked boxes forming their hideout.

"Hey, how do I get in there?" someone said.

"That sounded like Jeremy," Ron whispered.

"As much as I wish it were, I don't see how that's possible. It's got to be a trap," she whispered back.

"Where are you?" the voice said.

Alice and Ron didn't respond and remained perfectly still.

"I've got a date with Alice, and I've got at least a lifetime of points to pay Ron back," the voice said.

"It's got to be him," Ron whispered to Alice. "Who else would know that?"

"Theo was spying on us," she said.

"It's him," Ron said to Alice. "We're over here," he shouted and opened the concealed door to the hiding place.

Jeremy ran over to the entrance and gave them both a group hug. "You're not going to believe what happened on the Moon."

Dear Amy,

Sincerely trust you are feeling fine by now.
I am doing just that too. This is the life for me.
I'm sure about that now. Take care and enjoy the
remainder of your summer.

Love,
Zelda

ABOUT
THE
AUTHOR

Joey Rogers is an enthusiast of sci-fi, video games, and all-around geekery. He's a software developer by day in the high-tech city of Huntsville, Alabama and loves writing about what the future might hold. His first two novels are *An Alien, a Time Machine, and a Loser* and *An Alien, a Time Machine, and a Hero*.

Website: www.gegodyne.com
Twitter: @gegodyne
Email: gegodyne@gmail.com
Facebook: www.facebook.com/gegodyne

Made in United States
Orlando, FL
08 July 2024

48748550R00167